Fate is

Charles A. Robinson

Chapter 1

Fred Cosman leaned against the bitter November wind as he made his way across the parking lot. He had his head slightly bent forward and eyes squinted to battle the swirling snow assaulting his face. His left hand held a dark briefcase, a college graduation gift from his family. His right hand clasped his coat lapel against his neck. He took the stairs two at a time as he entered the D dock loading platform into the St. Paul, Minnesota main post office. He briskly walked by Anthon, a black mail handler loading trucks with outgoing mail.
"Hey Anthon" yelled Fred, "what's up?"
"Nothing much Fred, living the good life." Anthony smiled as he spoke.

Anthony (Anthon) Washington had been working on the D dock ever since he got discharged from the Army. Anthon was a big man with a gentle disposition and quick smile. Before the Army, he played offensive tackle for the Minnesota Gophers football team. An unfortunate knee injury sidelined his hopes of going pro. The beginning of his fall semester he felt compelled, like many, to join the service after the twin towers were hit on 9/11.

There wasn't anyone who didn't like Anthon. He was friendly, agreeable, and a great worker. Fred liked Anthon because he was the real thing. Nothing false about Anthon. What you see is what you get. No pretenses. It also helped that Anthon saved Fred's ass one night when Fred was getting mugged by three thugs. Fred had just started at the PO. Late one Friday night after work, Fred stopped for one too many at a local pub. Fred found himself in the wrong part of St. Paul at the wrong time. A little drunk and lost, Fred was easy prey for the local hoods. He was knocked down and getting robbed when Anthon happened by. Anthon had just come from a local bowling alley and turned a corner to find this commotion.

"What ya doing gents? Seems like ya have the odds wrong." That being said, Anthon picked up one of the thieves and hurled him into a dumpster. Then he grabbed another, lifted him off the ground like a pro wrestler would do, and slammed the thief into the ground. The other hood was so scared by this one-man army he took off running. Anthon picked up Fred, put him in a taxi, and sent him home. That was the first encounter Fred had with Anthon. Saved his butt and never gave his name. It was only when Fred decided to take a different way into the PO, by way of the D dock, that Fred learned Anthon was the guy who saved him. He couldn't thank Anthon enough, but Anthon just brushed it off as being nothing much. After Anthon saved Fred, Fred looked upon the dock worker as being special.

Fred had graduated from the University of Minnesota while working nights at the PO. The PO was just a means of paying for his education. He never gave much thought to those who worked on the docks or elsewhere. Felt they were working here just waiting for their pension. Fred always considered his employment with the PO to be a steppingstone to higher business. But Fred's attitude changed over the years. He was reminded that he had two brothers working for the PO, both were mail handlers. His father had been a postal clerk who retired after 30 years from the PO.

As Fred opened the door from the docks into the lobby, he heard a loud noise, and everything went black. When Fred woke up, he found himself on the floor up against the lobby wall. Smoke and debris were coming out of a large hole in the wall where the door used to be. Fred attempted to move, but his limbs didn't respond. There was ringing in his head and his vision was blurry. Slowly the feeling started to come back into Fred's arms and legs. He carefully stood, half stumbling backwards against the wall. His freshly pressed suit was wrinkled and dirty from the dust and smoke billowing out into the lobby. Fred stood there trying to make sense of what happened. The entire postal lobby was in chaos. Postal workers and customers were starting to move, brushing themselves off, helping one another to stand. Display racks with postal literature were knocked over, trash was all over the floor. A cloud of dusk lingered in the air.

Fred carefully made his way over to the gaping hole in the wall. He was dragging his left leg like a zombie. Leaning against the lobby wall, he looked into the hole to where the D dock should be. The area looked like a war movie. Equipment was tipped over; mailbags were thrown everywhere. Letters were still floating in the air through the dark smoke. Fred could hear people starting to moan and scream for help. He looked over to where Anthon was working…. nothing. Fred stumbled over mailbags and equipment, clawing his way to where he last saw Anthon. There, under an overturned mail cart, Fred saw Anthon. He quickly started pulling mailbags off Anthon, calling his name. "ANTHON! ANTHON!" When the bags were off, he looked down at the still body of Anthony Washington. Fred slowly sat backwards on the mail bags balancing himself with his left hand. With his right hand, he wiped his forehead. He was not believing what he saw.

Others came up behind Fred to help remove Anthon. It was then the reality of what happened struck Fred. An explosion! What the Post Office had been afraid of just happened, a terrorist bomb. A bomb had finally struck a federal building. Fred staggered over to a phone on the dock supervisors' desk and called upstairs to his office, the Office of Postal Inspector.

"Hello?" came a feminine voice.
"Ya, who's this?" Fred shouted into the phone.
"It's me Allie, that you Fred?"
"Allie", said Fred, "get Roy Downing and Chuck Yantz down to the D

dock pronto.......and oh ya, call the FBI!"
"What was that loud noise? Felt like a train hit the building."
"Allie! I don't have time to explain, just get Roy and Chuck down here now!"
"But whaa......t"

Fred hung up without waiting for a response and started to take in the scene around him. He was piecing together what had happened. It was definitely an explosion, but what caused it? He could smell burnt plastic and something almost like a sweet-smelling gunpowder. From his training at the Postal Inspector Academy in Potomac, Maryland, Fred remembered that smell......a bomb. During his training, Inspectors had to familiarize themselves with different kinds of explosives. Inspectors had to be knowledgeable about forensic evidence, and the smell of an explosion was one of them. Fred could never understand why the hell he had to know about explosives. He thought he'd be dealing with mail fraud, not bombs. Yet, as it was explained to the new recruits, a lot of armament was sent thru the mail. That included explosive. Fred didn't want to think it was a bomb, but...that smell.
"OK, clear the area right now! There may be a secondary explosion."
Workers started to run towards the nearest exit.... a large hole in the wall. Fred knew that if it was a bomb, there might be a second one to go off after a crowd gathered to maximize the carnage. Better to be safe.

"Hey Calhoun!" yelled Fred. The mail handler's union steward, Pat Calhoun, stopped and turned.
"Come over here, we're going to need you."
Calhoun gave a weary look and gave up on leaving the building to safety.
"What do you want Fred?"
"We're gonna need your help sorting out what happened here."
"Wait a minute, Fred. I'm a mail handler, not an inspector. This is your

job, not mine, and you're welcome to it. I'm going with the rest of the workers. Not gonna get my ass blown up for the PO....no sirrree." He started to turn away.

"Look Calhoun, you're not just a worker. You're a union steward, a representative for the mail handlers. Your union has a stake in this, and you're the closet representative of that union. It would be a shame if your union found out that one of their stewards didn't want to help find out how one of their union members was killed."

"Damn Fred, you don't play fair. What do you want me to do?"

"Look around. You know this dock well, see what's out of place, what's different, anything unusual."

"Unusual? Shit, look around, everything is unusual. D dock doesn't look like this every day."

"C'mon Calhoun, you know what I mean. Poke around, look for wires, burnt mailbags, that kinda stuff." Calhoun shuffled off to poke around.

The D dock was cleared of unnecessary personnel, and yellow police line tape was set up to block off the area. The first responders, EMTs, came and took the injured away. Poor Anthon was placed in a black bag and removed to the morgue. Five Postal Inspectors, along with the St. Paul police and FBI agents were scouting the D dock for any evidence. Fred walked by one of his colleagues.

"Find anything Roy?"

"Oh, some burnt canvas bags, half of a cell phone, could be a detonator, and some pieces of wire. That's about it so far. Gave it all to the FBI."

"The FBI? Why the hell did you give that shit to them? This is our territory. Those pricks will try to run this case."

"Fred! Those guys have greater resources then we do. Plus, they handle all kinds of cases like this. This is what they do! Now stop being territorial. Let's use their help and get this solved quickly. Don't be an ass!"

"I know, I know. You're right Roy. It's just that this is sort of personal. Anthon was a good guy."

"One of the best, Fred."

"You knew him?"

"Knew him? Hell, he was Godfather to my youngest, Katie."

"Get out! I didn't think you knew where the D dock was, let alone that you knew Anthon. How did you know him?"

"I wasn't always an Inspector. I used to do late night pick up of mailboxes. When I backed into the D dock with my truck, Anthon was always there with that big smile of his. Well, one night my wife called. She somehow got the D dock. Only Anthon was around. She asked for me, but I was out collecting mail. She told him she was in labor and had no way of getting to the hospital. She was in a bad way. Well, Anthon got in his car, drove to my house and took her to the hospital. He had to come back to work of course, but he got into all kinds of trouble. They wanted to fire him for walking off the job. I went and spoke to the supervisor, the Postmaster. They finally decided to give him a three-day suspension. I never forgot that. After my Katie was born, I ask Anthon to be her Godfather. He came to her birthday party every year. Katie loved him." Roy stopped talking and looked down. Fred could see he teared up a bit. Roy looked back up. "He was a hell of a man. He talked me into getting into management and then I went into the Inspection Service. All because of Anthon. I don't know how I'm gonna tell Katie."

Fred walked over to the dock supervisor's desk which was now the central gathering place for Fred's boss, Chief Inspector Mike White.

"Hi Fred" Mike said.

"Hi Mike. Sorry to bring you in on such a bad note."

"Well, we always felt it might happen after the Minneapolis riots, and it did. But why the PO? Surely there can be a better place to make a statement."

"I don't know," said Fred. "Maybe whoever did this was mad because they didn't get their TV Guide on time."

"Not funny Fred." Fred looked away.

"Well, what do we have so far Fred?" Mike waited for Fred's opinion.

"First, we know it was a homemade bomb because there was no metal involved. In fact, it seems whoever did this, did it with a sense of humor."

"What do you mean?" Mike said, puzzled by Fred's comment.

"Whoever it was used the same type of canvas material that the mail bags are made of."

"Anyway of finding out if a bag is missing?"

Fred smiled and pointed out that the post office goes through thousands of canvas bags each day and could never keep an inventory of where they all were.

"Hell, I bet there are some bags even in the locker rooms for sleeping on."

"Hey!" yelled Calhoun. "That's not right, you're making an accusation against professional clerks and mail handlers."

"Relax." Fred said. "Unless things have changed since I worked the night shift, the locker was always a place to catch a wink waiting for mail trucks to arrive. And since the supervisors never go in there, why change things? Besides, if someone naps on their lunch or break, who cares, right?"

"Ya, right." Calhoun echoed. "But who knows what shit management might do?"

"Don't be so sensitive Calhoun. I came from the docks, remember?"

Fred turned and walked towards the elevator for his office.

CHAPTER 2

Allie was bent over the lower file cabinet drawer as Fred entered the Inspectors Office.

"Mighty nice. .... work." Fred blurted out.

"Excuse me?" Allie said, unknowing what Fred referred to.

"The files." You have them in such great shape." Fred said with a smile.

Allie tilted her head slightly, gave Fred a quizzical look, and smiled.

"My files are not a subject for discussion. Say, what the hell was that noise and rumble? I swear it felt like the building was coming down. And look at you, did you have a late night? You're covered with dust, and your clothes are all wrinkled."

"There was an explosion on the D dock. The place is a mess down there."

Allie had a horrific look on her face. "Anybody hurt?"

Fred looked down, "ya, there's a mail handler guy name Anthon that was killed, a few others were injured." He dusted off dirt from his suit.

"Allie put her hand to her mouth, "Oh God, not Anthon!"

Fred turned to Allie, "Did you know him?"

"Know him? He trained me in my first few days before I was transferred inside to the floor. The supervisors didn't think a woman could handle lifting the mailbags. Oh Fred, he was such a nice man. Always a kind word and willing to help anybody."

Fred leaned against his desk and wiped his face with a tissue. "Seems like Anthon affected everybody he came in contact with."

Allie started to walk back towards her desk. "It's such a shame, I feel so bad for his wife."

Fred watched Allie leave. She was a single woman of thirty-four and she looked great A little over 5'4" with short blond hair and blue eyes. Ya, Allie looked fine. She definitely kept herself in shape. When Allie was on the workroom floor sorting mail, many guys made the mistake of hitting on her. Allie didn't take crap from any man. She usually had a quick retort to put a fellow in his place or make the other workers laugh at the poor fool who hit on her. A lot of guys sighed with despair when she got an office job upstairs. She was one of the few things that brightened up what otherwise would be a long dull night sorting mail.

Fred would have loved to take Allie out, but like the saying goes, 'Ya don't swim in the company pool." He also felt that professionally, it would be wrong to ask Allie out. However, many times Fred sensed that Allie was flirting with him. Or was it just his imagination? Thinking about asking Allie for a date was as far as he went. Having been divorced over a year, Fred would have liked to have a steady relationship. His career kept getting in the way, same as when he was married.

 He was getting coffee when Allie dropped a thick file on Fred's desk, startling him.
She looked at him. "Zimmerman case. You said you wanted to look it over today." Allie turned and walked out of his office. Fred picked up the file. Before he closed the door to his office, he caught a glimpse of Allie bending over to get more files. Fred thought, two times in one morning, things are looking up. He grabbed his coffee and went around to the other side
of his desk and sat down. He opened the folder and began reading.

Jack Zimmerman was a retail finance supervisor who came up short when a stamp assignment at a local store went bankrupt, owing the post office $6,000. Some stores would sell postal stamps to increase retail traffic in their stores. When the store got low on stamps, they would order more stamps from the post office. It seems that this store had two store outlets and the owner was doing badly. His sales were so low he decided to close the stores. Unfortunately for Zimmerman, the owner didn't notify the post office. It wasn't until a letter carrier told Zimmerman that the stores had suddenly closed that he was aware of the situation. The owner had declared bankruptcy and left town. Upper management felt the supervisor should have kept track of each postal assignment store even though Zimmerman had no knowledge that the stores had suddenly closed. Now, postal management was trying to get Zimmerman to cough up the $6,000. They felt that Zimmerman neglected his duties even though Zimmerman had sent registered letters of demand to the owner with no results. His attempts to attend the bankruptcy hearing were denied by postal management. The post office was holding Zimmerman responsible. It was Fred's job to make an inquiry to ensure there was no fraud. He had to interview Zimmerman and do an audit of his stamp inventory. In reality, Fred thought this was a bunch of bullshit. This was not the first time some store with a stamp consignment reneged on their contract. And it was not the first-time upper management tried to stick it to some poor schmuck. They were taking an easy way to recoup the lost $6,000 instead of going after the store owner. But this Zimmerman guy was fighting it. Hired his own lawyer to work with the supervisor's organization. This would definitely go to arbitration. Fred tossed the folder on the desk and leaned back. Good, he thought. He hoped the supervisor wins. If it all went down as written after a review, Fred would write a favorable report for the supervisor. The actions of upper management constantly irritated Fred. More than once, they threw supervisors under the bus. The supervisors had no union like the other employees to back them up, just a weak organization with no contract with the postal service. The postal clerks, the letter carrier's union, and all the other unions had specific contracts to argue a worker's case. Most times, upper management would cave into the unions to pacify them and keep from antagonizing union members. But supervisors were the lowest rung of management and subject to the whims of upper management who didn't have to deal with employees on the workroom floor. This was the main reason Fred refused every opportunity for promotions to upper management. He didn't like the bullshit and politics. Fred saw more supervisors, good men, quit the postal service and go into private industry. Many times, he was encouraged to get into upper postal management. No, Fred would stay with the inspection service, for now anyway.

CHAPTER 3

Wentworth Cosman made his way slowly up the concrete steps to his house on Skylark Street in St. Paul. The house was a single story, Craftsman-style house built with a detached garage during WWII. The neighborhood was a well-kept, established area of older homes. Wentworth's steps were slower than they use to be, his energy level depleted since the accidental death of his youngest son, Joey. It was an industrial accident as described by the post office. But Wentworth felt it was unsafe working conditions that killed his son. Joey was a gregarious person, always smiling, a fun type who lit up a room with his personality and made everyone comfortable being around him. Being the youngest of three kids, he naturally won the heart of his mother and the pride of his father. His older brothers, John and Fred, took Joey under their wing taking him hunting and fishing. The older brothers enjoyed the outgoing laid-back younger brother.

Wentworth was retired after 30 years of being a postal clerk. He then had more time to spend with his youngest son, a luxury he didn't have with the older two when he had been working. The loss of Joey seemed to age Wentworth. He just didn't seem to want to do much of anything. Most times he spent the days tinkering in the basement. At times he would stop, fooling himself that he heard Joey's voice.

Joey had just become engaged to his high school sweetheart and was working a lot of overtime at the post office to pay for a down payment on a house. One night while unloading trucks on the D dock, he moved the conveyor belt further into the semi-truck to get at the mailbags in the front half of the truck. As he bent down to push the start button for the conveyor, his shoulder length hair got caught in the chain and sprockets which turned the belt. His head was pulled with such force into the chain metal motor that it crushed the left side of his skull and partially lifted his scalp. Death was instantaneous. The official inquiry showed that the safety guard around the conveyor chain and motor had been removed. With the guard removed, the conveyor belt could be moved further into the truck, thereby allowing faster unloading of the mailbags. The mail handler's union yelled about unsafe working conditions and called the National Labor Relation Board and OSHA in to investigate.

After a month's investigation, a final report was presented to the post office management and the National Relations Labor Board. Although no evidence could prove who was responsible for removing the safety guard on the conveyor belt or when it was removed, the post office was found at fault because it had the ultimate responsibility of ensuring that all equipment used by employees was in proper working order before usage. OSHA cited the postal service for not providing a record showing the last inspection of the equipment. The fact the postal service did show a maintenance record didn't cut it with OSHA. The findings were adamant that all industrial equipment be inspected prior to use.

The more difficult part of this accident was the response from the mail handlers President, John Cosman, brother of Joey Cosman. John had been a constant critic of postal policies, whether they were justified or not. He opposed actions of management to change or modify any work rules or procedures. During contract negotiation, John would make 20 demands just to get one or two considered by management. He felt his approach would at least make management frustrated by his actions and agree to a few just to shut him up and get a contract signed. John had a way to pump up union members' energy, causing discontent on the workroom floor and the loading docks. He took common beefs that members had and turned those against the PO. To management, John was an agitator, someone who took satisfaction combating management in what he felt was postal mismanagement. Due to his aggressive approach, John was a suspect of any labor action during the uneasy negotiation period with the post office.

John was the oldest son of Wentworth Cosman. A great athlete in high school, he had the chance of both an academic and athletic scholarship to afford college. A smart kid, who people thought of as a natural leader. People seemed to look up to him. A friendly kid with an outgoing personality. John saw too many of his friends graduate from college with a large student loan debt only to end up with a dead-end job or unemployed living in their parent's basement. Being a smart kid, he decided to work and make some money. However, he decided to first join the Marine Corps for a few years. After he got out, his father encouraged him to work for the post office until John was ready to make a permanent decision. So, John took the postal exam, getting ten points for being a veteran, and obtained a position. He felt good about making money and enjoyed his job as a mail handler. Yet his aversion to authority that developed in the military caused him to question what he thought were boneheaded policies of postal management. As time went by, he became more anti-management and spoke out at union meetings. Like his dad, he eventually became a Union president. Unlike his dad, John became a thorn in the side of postal management. Whereas his father would seek a middle ground, John would press an issue to the extreme. In one labor grievance, an employee was charged with threatening a supervisor. The employee went after the supervisor, chasing him around a desk. The employee struck the supervisor several times until he was subdued by other employees. During the grievance, John stipulated that the supervisor escalated the conflict by not running away and isolating himself in an office. This would've given the employee time to cool down and the issue could have been resolved. This outlandish argument was overshadowed by the grievance board considering John's proposal. The employee was eventually found at fault and discharged for attacking another employee.

Yet the consideration of John's argument highlighted the mistrust towards the grievance board. Many felt the board awarded arguments on the basis of who won the previous grievance. It was almost like the board granted decisions in turn for management and the unions. If management was awarded a decision, the next decision would be awarded to the union. There seemed to be no logical reason for some decisions. In one situation, an employee threatened a manager that he'd shove a bowling ball down the manager's throat. The fact that this was physically impossible, did no good. The employee was given a one-day suspension. No one could believe the grievance board's decision. It didn't make sense. The decision gave credence to the idea that the grievance board was just appeasing management and the union instead of basing an issue on its merits.

John used this mistrust to his benefit. He thew numerous accusations into an argument hoping that something would stick, if for no other reason, than it muddied the true issue. John won many decisions. He won not because of the argument or issue, but more because postal management saw no good in drawing out an issue and possibly upsetting union members. The postal service wouldn't be going out of business because of a lost grievance. The main concern was to keep the mail moving.

It wasn't until John's youngest brother, Joey, was killed at work that John became more aggressive and anti-management. To John, everything was a safety issue endangering the wellbeing of employees. He filed grievance after grievance from floors not swept more frequently to leaking faucets in the restrooms. It seemed that John would do anything to battle management. Larger issues of safety and discipline involved heated arguments at labor negotiations. He wanted someone's head on a platter for the death of his brother. He even charged that management had blood on their hands, charging the postal service with murder. John was in the headlights of management and the postal inspection service after the explosion on D dock

CHAPTER 4

Each Sunday, dinner was a requirement at the Cosman household.   It didn't matter that their two sons were grown men with lives of their own. Their mother expected them to be there. They may be grown men, but they were still her boys. This became more important since the death of her youngest boy, Joey.   The dinner was always served around noon so that the boys and ol'man Cosman could watch the Vikings football team on the television afterwards. For the past few years, the loud cheering and bantering in the living room was more subdued. It just didn't seem the same without Joey around.

Fred parked his Volvo in the driveway. He saw the silver Ford F-150 which indicated that his brother John was already there. The brothers always got along, but the last few years put a strain on their relationship.   John seemed to initiate comments against Fred because he considered Fred to be part of management. Any chance to take a swipe against management, John would aim it at his brother. Even though Fred never considered himself as part of management, it bothered him that John directed his comments towards him. The Sunday dinner became a chore for Fred instead of a family gathering. He didn't like being hassled by John, he was weary of his mother always mentioning Joey like he was still there, and he didn't like his father's depressed demeaner. It seemed that Joey dying took the life out of the family.

Fred went through the back door into the kitchen and could smell the pork smoked shoulder cooking in the oven. Pots were bubbling on the stove, some had steam coming up from under the lids. It was a small kitchen, more utilitarian for cooking than for sitting in. He loved his mother's cooking and was always rewarded with a large doggie bag when he left. The meat was the main item, backed up with at least four to five vegetables. When they eventually sat down for dinner, it looked like a Norman Rockwell painting. His mother was standing by the stove in her usual attire, a housedress with a flower print apron that hung from the neck down to her knees and tied in the back. The apron had two front pockets from which his mother would extract a handkerchief or tissue to wipe his nose or face when he was small. She would take it out, wet it with a bit of spit, and wipe the dirty mark off his face. In later years, Fred figured that it must be a mother thing because all his friends mothers did the same thing. Even now Fred could see the corner of a tissue peeking up from the pocket, ready for action.

"Hi Mom."

Fred's mother turned with a big smile, "Fred!" She put down the wooden spoon she used to stir the gravy and walked over to him for hug. "You're just in time, dinner will be ready in fifteen minutes. Go in and join your brother and father, they're watching the game pre-show. I really don't know why they bother with that; the game is not for another hour and a half."

Fred smiled. He could see that in her day she was a beautiful woman. Even now with wrinkles and gray hair, she looked good. Fred walked into the living room and grabbed a few potato chips out of the bowl in front of John.

"Hey Sport! How's it going? Much happening up on management row?"

"Hi John." Fred thought to himself, right off the bat with the comments, this might end up being another agonizing Sunday. Fred smiled, "How are things down in the dungeon?"

"Hi Dad, how you are feeling?"

"I'm OK Fred, I have my good days and I have my bad ones, just like everyone else."

"You see any of your old buddies down at Murphy's Bar?"

"Naw, just don't feel like being around all those old farts jabbering about the old days. I don't wish to live through them again, once was enough."

Hell, Dad I thought you liked yakking it up with your old work friends. Does Mark Sullivan still go there?"

"Mark Sullivan died a few years back from cancer. Besides all they talk about is the same old stuff. I've heard those stories four or five times. That is all they live for, telling those damn stories."

"Oh! Sorry Dad, I didn't know about Sullivan. That's a shame, I liked Sullivan. Didn't you two start working on the docks at the same time? Wow, cancer huh, bad thing that shit."

"Well, he's at peace now and doesn't have to listen to that nagging wife of his. I wonder who's ear she's gonna torture now? So, there is a blessing in dying Fred."

John spoke up. "So big postal inspector, any news on the explosion on the D dock? Any hapless employee get charged?"

"We're still working on it. Waiting for the FBI forensic report to come in. The D dock is a total mess. It's amazing that more people weren't killed. We even had some customers hurt that were standing in the lobby next to D dock."

Ol'man Cosman fidgeted in his chair. "Can't you two find something else to talk about?"

"Ya, sure Dad" Fred said, and sat down at the other end of the couch John was on. He reached for a few more chips when his mother yelled in from the kitchen.

"Don't you guys munch too much on those chips, dinner will be ready soon. Wentworth come out here and carve the pork smoked shoulder."

"No rest for the weary boys." Their father got up slowly, rearranged the slippers on his feet, and shuffled into the kitchen.

"Dad's moving a bit slower these days," Fred said.

"Ya, age is catching up with the ol'boy. Plus, he's never been the same since Joey got killed." Fred started to make a face but bit his tongue a little.

"It was an accident, John; an industrial accident and you know it."

"Is that what they're feeding you up there on management row? That your kid brother's death was an accident? Oh, excuse me...an industrial accident. What a bunch of crap that is. You think that safety guard came off by itself? Huh? Someone in management took that off so the mail handlers would work faster! That's the hard truth!" By now John was up on his feet and walking back n' forth, agitated. Fred was looking down feeling exhausted. He hated these moments with his brother. There were times he almost made excuses not to attend these dinners, but he knew his mother would be extremely disappointed not to have both her boys there.

"Look John, I didn't come here to argue with you. Do you have to turn every conversation into a battle?"

"When you side with management and go against the family I do." Now Fred was on his feet. Even though John was older, Fred was a bit taller, but John had the psychological edge. Each was now in the others personal space, and neither was backing off. Their father poked his head into the living room and saw that the boys might go at it.

"Ok guys, knock it off. This is still my house, and you'll respect that. Now go sit in the dining room, we're about to eat." When all the food was brought in, everyone sat down. They held hands and said grace together. Fred could feel the strength of his brother's hand. He remembered how John used those hands to pull him out of the Mississippi River when he was twelve. They were playing on the ice at Thanksgiving and Fred fell through. One-minute John wasn't there and the next he had Fred by the collar. John got Fred home without their parents knowing what happened. Fred put on dry clothes and put the wet ones in the wash pile. So, at this moment Fred had to remember that John was still his brother, a jerk at times but still his brother. After the dinner and game, Fred was ready to leave.

"Mom where's Dad? I want to say goodbye."

"Oh, he went down to his man cave in the basement. I swear he has been spending too much time down there. It's almost like he was hiding from the world."

Fred made his way down the narrow basement stairs. It was just like the basement in many craftsman- style homes; low head clearance, large stone walls, not poured cement but large stones stacked on top of one another. Probably put there in the 1920s. Unlike most basements of that era, this one was void of that damp odor, this one was dry. Fred noticed a strange smell.

"Geez Dad you got some funky smell going on down here, what the hell is that?" Wentworth Cosman quickly threw a towel onto his work bench project.

""Oh, Fred, you startled me a bit."

"Whatcha working on Dad?"

"Oh, just fixing an old radio from back in the day."

"Dad, what's that smell?"

"The smell? I found a dead rat down here a few days back, got rid of it then sprayed some Lysol disinfectant on the spot. Guess it still smells a bit, I just don't notice it anymore."

"Ok, I just wanted to say goodbye, give me a hug here, good luck with your project." Fred went back up to the kitchen where his mother handed him a Tupperware container of food.

"You heat that up tomorrow night for dinner; it'll warm you right up." She patted him lovingly on the shoulder. He kissed his mother and shook John's hand.

"No hard feelings Sport?"

"No, we're good John. I just don't like arguing with you."

"I know Sport. It's just sometimes I get pissed at what happened to Joey. It was senseless. And I know I can be hard at times. It's just my nature. But you're still my brother and I love ya."

"Same goes here guy, take care of yourself."

As Fred backed out of the driveway, he looked up at the living room window. There was his mother waving goodbye to him. She did that ever since he first started school, from the first grade on up. She always stood by the window watching her boys go out into the world.

Fred smiled as he headed southwest to his condo in Minneapolis, a good twenty-minute drive.

CHAPTER 5

When Fred walked into his office, he found Mike White sitting there drinking a cup of coffee and reading a report.

"Well, Mike you're up and at 'em early this Monday morning."

"Ya, I just couldn't sleep so I decided to get the day started. We got the forensics back from the FBI lab."

"Anything we can use? Any prints, serial numbers?"

"Afraid not Fred. Says here it was a total amateur that concocted this bomb up. Kinda like the ones back in the sixties with the anti-war protestors, The Underground Weathermen."

"The who?"

"The Underground Weathermen. They were a splinter group of the SDS, Students for a Democratic Society, which conducted protests against the Vietnam War. The Weathermen were more like a radical left organization. The Underground Weathermen started in the Ann Arbor, Michigan University campus. The group launched a bombing campaign against the establishment, from about 1969 till 1975. They targeted police buildings, the US capitol, the Pentagon, mostly government buildings. Their goal was to kill police officers and military personnel in an attempt to cause a violent overthrow of the US government. Two of the more outspoken members were a Bill Ayers and a Bernadine Dohrn. I believe they got married and went into hiding. Dohrn was put on the FBI's most wanted list. Dohrn was quoted as saying 'You don't need to be a Weatherman to know which way the wind is blowing. I guess that's how they got their name. Oddly enough, later Bill Ayers was a big supporter of Barack Obama. The Weathermen eventually broke into splinter groups, and just kinda faded from what I know."

"Sooo, Mike, what is your point?"

"My point is that the bomb makings are the same as the one that went off on D dock."

"But Mike, why the post office? What the hell does mail have to do with bombing?"   "Not sure Fred. Maybe it's tied in with that Antifa group that's been rioting in Minneapolis. They're pretty much left-wing radicals from what I can see. Their motive seems the same...... cause unrest. Who knows?"

"Well, it seems like quite a leap from breaking windows to bombing buildings."

"Not really Fred. I mean that ANTIFA group tried to burn down a police station in Seattle, Washington with people inside. Crazy people do crazy things."

"So, what? You figure it might've been a radical group?"

"Who knows Fred? Like I said, people with an agenda do weird shit to promote their cause."

"I don't know Mike. Bombing a post office doesn't make sense. You would think that anyone with a beef against the establishment would pick a police station or a military type of installation."

"Could be Fred, could be. At any rate, let's keep an open mind and track down leads as they come in. Get in touch with that agent James over at the FBI. See if they've got a list of people who've been on their radar causing problems. It might shake someone out."

"Ya Mike. I guess it couldn't hurt."

Mike sipped the last of his coffee and put his cup on the desk and walked out.

"ALLIE!" Fred yelled through the open door.

Allie walked in. "Yes Fred?"

"Say, see if you can get an agent James over at the FBI office on the phone."

"OK." Allie turned around and went out. Fred leaned back, put one foot up on his desk and began looking through the FBI forensic report

CHAPTER 6

It was around two in the afternoon when Fred headed out of the post office parking lot. He angled over to 35E highway and drove up to Hwy 694 for the 30-minute ride to the FBI office in Brooklyn Center. After showing his credentials to the security guard, he entered the building. He walked to the elevator and pressed the up button. Fred looked around and smiled. He thought, what is up with these FBI people? This place is spotless, like it has never been used.   The elevator door opened, Fred walked in and pushed the button for the sixth floor. On the sixth floor he found the office of Special Agent In-charge James. He opened the door and walked in. It was a new office, in a new building, not like the archaic structure from the 1930s that Fred worked out of. The office had modern furniture, lighting, all the trappings of an agency that had an exceptionally large budget. Behind the shapely desk was a just as shapely secretary. The name plate on the desk was Miss Sullivan.   The secretary looked up and smiled as Fred came in.

"Good morning, may I help you?"

"Yes, good morning. I'm here to see Agent James."

"Certainly, may I have your name?"

"Cosman, Fred Cosman." He looked at the women's name plate. "Say, you wouldn't possibly related to a guy named Sullivan who worked for the post office, would ya?"

"Why yes, he was my father, did you know him?"

"Umm a little bit. He worked with my ol'man."

The women looked up, "Oh really?"

"Ya, I'm surprised you didn't end up working there. Seems like many families do."

"No, I got this job right out of college. I enjoy it."

"Well, alright Ms. Sullivan."

Fred walked in after being announced. Agent James was an older gentleman, a career FBI agent. He sported some girth around his middle, but James was stocky, not fat. His forearms were huge, and he looked like he could take care of himself in a fight. The sleeves of his white shirt were rolled up to his forearm, and his tie was pulled a bit away from his neck.

"So, how can I help you Mr. Cosman?"

"Please, make it Fred. When I hear Mr. Cosman, I think of my father." James smiled. "Ok Fred, what can I do for ya?"

"I'm investigating a bombing at the St. Paul Post Office three weeks ago. You guys were good enough to provide a forensic report from the remnants we sent over of cell phone parts found at the site." Fred took out his notepad and a pen.

"Ya, I'm familiar with that. So, are you the lead investigator on that? We were instructed to assist your office on that case, you know since 9/11, interagency cooperation and all that." Fred looked up.

"This kinda fell in my lap. I was at the post office D dock when the bomb went off. We were hoping that the FBI may have some leads on possible suspects."

"Wow, no kidding, you were there, huh? Well, we're always trying to stay ahead of things and constantly compiling lists of possible people or organizations that have been showing up on the radar. You know, people with known terrorist ties or just domestic groups kicking up a fuss, that kind of thing. Lately Antifa has come under scrutiny because of the riots in Minneapolis. Sometimes we get minor players who have the potential to become militant."

"Anybody stand out James?"

"Mmm..." James paused. "Naw, not yet, but there's always someone that pops up. It's a matter of time. However, like the report states, whoever did this was definitely an amateur."

"That's the second time I've heard that." Fred said.

"What?"

"That's the second time I heard that it was probably an amateur. I mean how can you guys be so sure?"

James got up from his desk, got a cup of coffee and came back.

"You want some coffee?" Fred said no thanks without looking up. James sat back down and continued.

"Amateurs have a way of doing things. They're sloppy, they cut wires too long or too short, use too much tape. Whereas an expert, now they're good. Everything is neat, precise, packaged well for maximum effect."

Fred stopped writing in his notepad and looked up. "Sounds like you admire them, and how do you know so much about the pros?"

"Spent three tours in Iraq with a Marine bomb squad. Those insurgent SOBs could put a bomb together with gum and tape and make it small and neat. Ya could barely detect anything. But I got good at noticing small things. Different color dirt surrounded by a darker color. Maybe too many concrete building blocks where there shouldn't be any, small things. Anyway, after we exploded them, we could see how the bombs were made up. Some of those Iraqis had a certain manner of constructing a bomb. Sort of like a signature, that's what I noticed."

Fred was almost staring. "Damn, I didn't think there was that much to bomb construction."

"Oh ya. And I'll tell ya another thing. Whoever did that was probably left-handed." In disbelief, Fred put his notepad on James's desk.

"Wait a minute. You're telling me you can tell if the bomb maker was a lefty or righty? How?"

"Easy. It's the way they twist the wires together. Ya see, a righty will twist wires clockwise. Whereas most times a lefty will twist wires counterclockwise."

"For real?"

"Sure. You ever try to untie a loaf of bread? You keep twisting it to open, but the wrapper gets tighter. Chances are it was tied by a lefty. Frustrating as hell to those of us who are right-handed. Ya just wanna make a sandwich, but ya can't untie the bread wrapping. Pisses ya off. Fred, you have a greater probability that the bomb maker was a lefty.

And that's a great clue."

"Anything else you can tell me?"

"You most likely already know that the cell phone is a snitch and ditch. Probably stolen from Kmart, Walmart, or some retail store with the intent of never using it for calling. If you're canvassing neighborhoods, look for a lefty and someone who bought low voltage wire like the kind for taillights or a trailer. Also, someone who purchased Cyanoacrylate glue, commonly called crazy glue. The glue helps piece the wires together better."

"So, that's it huh? No package wrapping?"

"Actually, there is. We found a burnt brown paper wrapping. We know from the markings that it was the package that contained the bomb. And guess what? There was an address. The package was being sent to 727 Orient Street, Northwest, St. Paul.

"Hey! That's great. All we have to do is find out who the recipient was."

Nope that's not gonna do us any good Fred."

Fred looked surprised. "Why not?"

"The package was addressed to a J. D. Cooper."

"Why, what's the matter with that?"

Agent James held up the burnt wrapping as if it was show and tell time. "Think of it Fred. A package is addressed to a J. D. Cooper, at 727 Orient Street, Northwest.

"So?"

"Ah, maybe you're too young to remember, but back in the early seventies there was a plane hijacked. Some guy was going to blow up the plane unless he got a ransom. He eventually got $200,000, then parachuted out of the plane. Not he nor the money were ever found."

"James, where the hell are you going with this?"

"The hijacker's name was J.D. Cooper, right? The plane was a Northwest Orient, Boeing 727. Get it?"

"No."

"Fred. The name, J.D. Cooper was on the package. The address number was 727, as in Boeing 727. The street was Orient Street Northwest, as in Northwest Orient."

"No shit? How the hell did ya figure that one out?"

"Well, it took some head scratching, but there was something about the name and address that seemed familiar to me. I ran my idea by some of the older FBI agents and they agreed that it made sense. I admit that it's an educated guess at best, but it fits."

"James, why would someone use that name and address?"

"Not sure Fred. Maybe it's the time frame thing. Maybe, the person who sent the bomb had a thing about 1971. Maybe it's a statement thing, an act against a symbol of the establishment. In this case we think maybe someone may eventually ask for a ransom or there will be more bombings. Who knows? That's all I got for now Fred."

"You've been a great deal of help James. Thanks for seeing me."

"No problem Fred, always good to help another agency."

"Anything else?"

"Well, we have a name or two that just came to us." James hesitated.

"Tell ya what. I'll keep you posted if we find out anything else."

Fred closed his notepad, put his pen away, got up, and walked out.

"Good afternoon Ms. Sullivan."

"Good afternoon inspector."

After Fred left, Agent James gave one curious look out the office to where Fred had left. Then he got on the phone to Chief Inspector Mike White at the St. Paul Post Office.

CHAPTER

Fred was only back in his office for ten minutes when he got a call from his boss, Mike White.

"Hi Mike. I just got back from the FBI office. What's up?"

"There has been another bombing."

"Aw damn. Where abouts?"

"It's the Minneapolis Post Office on 1st Street South. Get your coat back on and meet me downstairs in fifteen minutes."

"On my way boss."

"Oh Fred. I decided to take Inspector Roy with us, he'll meet you in the lobby."

"Roy? Why ya bring him?"

"Well, we're gonna need more manpower and ah......he's already somewhat familiar with the case. I briefed him while you were gone. Besides, another set of eyes is always good."

Fred was a little puzzled when he hung up the phone.

It was a thirty-minute ride up Highway 52 and over to Interstate 94. The Minneapolis Post Office sat on the banks of the Mississippi River on the West River Parkway side. From the top floor of the building, one could view the St. Anthony Falls lock and dam. It was a genuinely nice location for any building.

All three inspectors got out of the postal car and headed to the back of the post office. A small crowd was milling around a destroyed postal truck. Yellow tape marked off a large area surrounding the vehicle. Firemen were rolling up fire hoses and loading them onto the fire truck. Inspector White approached a postal security guard holding a clipboard and talking on the phone.

"You in charge here?" White said to the guard.

"Ya, Bob Foss. And you be?"

"Postal Inspector White. This is Inspector Cosman and Downing." The men nodded to the security guard.

"What do we have here?"

"We have two dead, three injured, a blown-up truck and mail all over the place. The EMTs are working on the injured now. The driver was inside the post office when the truck exploded. That's about it. I called the fire department in case there was a secondary fire from the embers. They snuffed out the embers with some dry chemical stuff. Unfortunately, that was after they had deployed the hoses. Now the poor bastards have to load the hoses back up without using them."

"Well, that's good Bob. That way we don't have to shift through wet mail."

"Ok. Fred, why don't you and Roy go over to the truck and assess the situation? Formulate what you think we have to do. See if you're able to get a statement from the injured. I'll stay here and call Agent James over at the FBI and then go over what Bob here has written down."

The two inspectors headed towards the truck. Inspector White got out his cell phone.

"Hello, Agent James here."

"James hi, this is Inspector White. Say, we had another bombing over at the Minneapolis Post Office. Doesn't look good. I was wondering if we could get your forensic team down here?"

"Another bombing, huh? Well, whoever is doing this didn't wait too long. I'll send my team right over."

"Great. We really appreciate your help."

"Say White, is that fellow Cosman with you?"

"Ya. Him and another Inspector, Inspector Downing. Is there a problem?"

"Not really, just what I talked with you about on the phone."

"Look! Cosman is a good Inspector, top shelf. I know what you said, but I have the greatest confidence in him, regardless of who he's related to."

"Ok, just wanted to be sure we're on the same page."

"Damn, you old timers look at everything."

"Me? Old timer? Look it White, you're no spring chicken yourself. I bet when you fart dust comes out."
White chuckled as he closed out the call.

The Inspectors went over the damaged truck, assessed the damage. and got a statement from the driver and the two injured employees. They put that together with the statement from the postal security guard Bob Foss. The FBI forensic team wouldn't be done for another two hours so the inspectors headed back to the St. Paul Post Office. Roy Downing had gone home for the day, while White and Fred hung around and talked a bit more about the bombings.
"What do ya think Fred? Any ideas about who's behind these bombings?"
"According to what Agent James said, it could be Antifa, domestic terrorists or some character who has a beef with the world. Or maybe all three. Might be somebody within Antifa acting alone being a domestic terrorist, or a lone wolf type."
Mike spoke up." Whoever it is seems to be familiar with postal route operations."
"What makes ya say that, Mike?"
"I don't know, just a feeling. Bear with me on this. The bombs were delivered by postal trucks. The first one went off shortly after being dropped off. The second one exploded while it was still in the truck. Maybe whoever did this, didn't want anyone to be hurt. They just wanted to destroy property."
"But people were hurt. Hell, Anthon was killed and two others plus we have injured employees."
"I know, I know. It might have been a bad timing issue. Maybe the detonator went off at the wrong time. Maybe it was defected. Remember. We're dealing with the work of an amateur. Somehow, I think it is a person who knows postal routing operations. Just a gut feeling."
"Well Mike, you've always been good about smelling these things out."
Rubbing his forehead, Mike gave out a small sigh. Yaaa? Well, maybe

my sixth sense is getting rusty. In the meantime, I need you to close out those two cases you were working on before these bombings occurred."

"What?" Mike, don't ya think this is a bad time to divert me from the bombing? Didn't ya say we needed more manpower on this case?"

"I did Fred. But the world doesn't stop because of one or two events. Those other cases are going to arbitration, and we need to close them out with our report. Besides, I have Roy, Chuck, and others working on the bombings as well. Plus, we enlisted the help of the FBI. Trust me on this Fred. I can spare you for a little bit. It shouldn't take you long. Let's call it quits for the night. The wife is going to be pissed that I'm late for dinner again."

Fred hesitantly walked to the car as he started to turn and speak, he thought better of it and got in.

CHAPTER 8

Instead of going home, Fred drove over to Murphy's Bar & Grill. He felt after his talk with Mike, he needed a drink. As he pulled in front of the bar, Fred thought, what a seedy looking place. The outside had a seventies brick façade, with small rectangular windows on each side of the entrance. Dirty white curtains allowed light to come out, but no one could see in. He walked through the door and looked around. The place hadn't changed much except for the patrons. Murphy's had always been a watering hole for postal employees, active and retired. Over the bar hung an Old Hamm's Beer neon light. Fred always remembered looking at the white bear in the sign. On his day off, ol'man Cosman took his son to the bar. He sat Fred on a bar stool with an ice-cold coke, a bag of chips, and the best tasting hot dog Fred ever tasted. Actually, the hot dog wasn't much, but being there with his dad made the hot dog taste great. Back in those days there was sawdust on the floor to prevent anyone from slipping on spilled beer. The place still smelled the same and the walls were slightly yellow from years of guys smoking. A couple of stuffed deer heads were mounted on the walls. There was the slight sound of polka music coming from the aged juke box. Ya, a midwestern bar couldn't get much more....... midwestern.

Fred recognized a few old timers sitting at a round table over in the corner. He recognized a few of his dad's cronies and walked over. "Hello Jack, Sven, Henry."

All three guys looked up. Slapping the table with his fingers, Sven spoke first. "Holy buckets, looks vat da cats dragged in. How ya been munchkin? Haven't seen yas since yas was no taller thana' a cows teat."

Fred smiled and sat down.

"Well, you're still the same charming Swede."

"Ya, that I am Freddie, that I am."

Jack spoke up. "Oh, hell Fred, Sven couldn't charm a mouse even if he had cheese in his hand. "Ohhhhh, says you?"

"Ya, says me, ya damn ol'potato eater." Both men smiled.

Fred smiled at Jack. "So, how ya been Jack, long time."

"Yep, long time since clear blue waters." Jack was referring to the old Hamm's Beer commercials that stated that the beer was made from clear blue waters. "So, what brings ya back to this old place?"

"Ah, I just got off work and needed a drink and thought I might see my Dad here or maybe my brother John."

"Your Dad? Hell, he hasn't been here for a few years. The last time I saw him was at Sullivan's funeral. By the way, how's your Dad doing?"

"He's doing Ok, I guess. He hasn't been the same since Joey's death. Seems like it took the spark out of him." The waitress came by and took Fred's order, and the others bought another pitcher of beer.

Sven spoke out. "Ya, that yas a bad thing, that. Ve'alls felt really sad about dat Freddie." Sven was the only friend of his father that called him Freddie.

Jack turned to Fred. "Say, I heard your brother has been taking some heat from postal management. He's still feels that management covered up Joey's accident. He called them murderers and such."

"I know Jack. John can be hot headed at times."

"Sure, Fred but if I was him, I'd watch what I say."

"Why? What do ya mean?"

"Well, it's none of my business mind ya, but he was overheard saying that whoever bombed the post office should get a medal. And that's not good to be spreading around these days."

"Get out! Really?"

"There's been talk Fred. There's been talk."

"Talk huh?"

Fred chatted a bit more with his dad's old cronies. Sitting back, Fred thought, his father was right, all these guys talk about are the old times. But then again, why not? What else do you talk about when you're retired? Fred finished his beer. It was snowing a little when he left Murphy's Bar. On the way back to his apartment, Fred mulled over what Jack repeated about John saying give the bomber a medal. Fred knew that was not good for John. That would surely bring the attention of the FBI and the Postal Inspection Service. It might also bring unwanted attention on Fred who was investigating the bombings. Could that be why Mike brought Roy and Chuck in on the case? Is that why Mike told him to work on these other two cases? Was he, himself, a potential suspect? Fred also remembered something......John was a lefty.

CHAPTER 9

Allie was already in the office when Fred arrived. He still had some snow on his shoulders which he brushed off.

"Still snowing out there huh?"

"Ya, the WCCO weatherman said it may stop around noon, but you know weathermen. It's snowing lightly, but not much is sticking. Just a bunch of slush splashing up onto your windshields."

"You want some coffee, Fred? I just made a batch."

"Ohhh, I'd love a cup." Allie poured Fred a cup and brought it over to his desk. "Keep it coming, I want to get those two arbitration cases done so I can work on those bombings."

Allie turned and looked at Fred.

"What? Do I have more snow on me?"

"Don't you know?"

"Know what Allie?"

"Mike White is having a meeting in his office right now about the bombings. Roy is in there, Chuck, and that FBI Agent James. I thought you knew about it."

Fred sat back in his chair trying to look nonchalant. "Ya, must've forgot about it. Mike asked me to get these cases done and then to join them."

Allie shrugged her shoulders and said, "Ok."

Fred could feel the anger building up inside. What the hell is going on he thought. Am I being pushed out of my own case? Am I being overly sensitive? He swirled his chair around and looked out the window and looked at the St. Paul skyline. He just didn't feel good about this. Something's not right. What were his options? He could storm into White's office and demand to know what was going on. That would be a rookie mistake and bad for the career or he could finish the two cases and join the team. He decided on a third option, he had to talk to his brother John.

Fred worked late trying to finish up the two arbitration cases. Allie had left hours ago, leaving a fresh pot of coffee going on the Mr. Coffee. Fred stretched his arms over his head and straightened his back to loosen the back muscles. He put his pen down and turned and looked out his window. It was dark outside, and the lights of St. Paul made a picturesque view. He looked at the cars driving around on the streets below. The snow had stopped, and the landscape below was a picture portrait of a large city after a snowfall. He figured that John's union meeting would be breaking up now and the members would be milling around the bar. Fred squared up the papers he was working on and put them in a folder. He walked over, shut off the Mr. Coffee, turned the lights off, grabbed his coat, and left.

The Gallagher Hansen VFW Post 295 was a ten-minute ride from the St. Paul Post Office. The roads were fairly good, and the traffic was light. Getting to the VFW Post, he parked in back and went in. Fred was never one for joining the VFW Post, American Legion, or any other military-related organization. He thought of them as just another bar where guys went and swapped stories, pretty much like the guys at Murphy's Bar. A Toby Keith song was coming out of speakers hidden somewhere. Fred spotted his brother John leaning against the bar talking with some guys. One still had his postal uniform on. Fred walked over.

"Hi John!"

John turned and put his beer down.

"Hey Fred. What brings you down here?"

"Ah……I was working late. Say, you have a few minutes? I'd like to talk to ya."

"Sure. Anything wrong? Mom, Pop they, Ok?"

"Oh sure, they're fine. I just wanted to get your thoughts on something." Fred ordered a beer and both men walked over to an empty corner table.

"So, what's up that you need to pick the brains of your big brother?"

"Look. I've been working on these two postal bombings and I'm getting some strange vibes."

"Sounds intriguing." John took a sip of his beer.

"No seriously. I've been working on these bomb cases. The other day out of the blue my boss, Mike White, brought in two other inspectors. Said we needed more manpower, more eyes on the case and all that bullshit. Said he wanted me to wrap up two other ongoing cases that were going to arbitration."

John looked at Fred. "So, what's wrong with that? Seems reasonable to me."

"Well, today when I came into the office to work on the cases, I found out that White was having a meeting about the bombings with the other two inspectors and an FBI agent helping us."

"Ya? So?"

"John. He didn't even mention it to me. I had no idea he was having a meeting. Had to find it out from my secretary."

John got a smile on his face and a gleam in his eyes. "Ah ya…. Allie. The guys sure miss her down on the workroom floor. Hell, we all do. She had a way of………."

"John! I'm trying to tell you something!"

"Ok, Ok, you don't have to bite my head off."

"Sorry. It's been a long day and I'm tired." Fred took a sip of beer. "The other day after work I needed a drink, so I stopped by Murphy's Bar."

"Damn! That old place? Say do they…"

"John! For Christ's sake, will you listen up?" John stopped cold and put his beer down.

"Like I said. I stopped by Murphy's for a drink. I ran into the Swede, Jack, and what's his name…." Fred snapped his fingers trying to remember. "Henry! Ya, Henry. You know, Dad's old buddies? Well after a while, Jack said something strange. He mentioned that he heard you're catching some heat from postal management. Those were his exact words, catching some heat from postal management." John straightened up in his chair and stared at Fred.

"Jack said you were heard saying that management basically had blood on their hands. That whoever bombed the post office should be given a medal."

John was just staring at Fred. In a cold voice he said, "So, what are you investigating me now?"

"No, no John, that's not it. What I'm saying is, put all the pieces together. Me, being kinda edged out of the investigation, you supposedly being in trouble with postal management and your alleged comments. I don't know, something's in the wind."

John pushed his chair back, got up, and grabbed his coat.

"Look Fred, I don't give a rat's ass what postal management thinks or believes. All I know is that they killed Joey and covered it up. Called it an industrial accident. They can call it whatever they want. But maybe. Just maybe, the postal chickens have come home to roost! And as for you, I don't give a rat's ass what you think or believe either." Sarcastically John said, "See ya Sunday!" He abruptly walked out.

Fred sat there. He felt exhausted, both physically and mentally. It had been a long day and there was a lot of information to process. He felt John acted a bit defensive, more than he should. He also noted that John held the beer glass in his left hand. Fred was deflated. He didn't want to think what he was thinking. He needed to close the two cases he had been working on all day and get back on the bombing investigations.

CHAPTER 10

It was a week away from Thanksgiving and there was another
attempted bombing. Only this time nothing happened. The package
with the bomb had the wrapping fall apart and was discovered by a
clerk. She noticed wires hanging out of the package and called her
supervisor who in turn called the St. Paul Police Department. They
sent over a bomb squad to disarm the bomb. The Inspection Service
got involved and sent it to the FBI forensic lab. They were waiting on a
report.

Mike White was getting pressured from Postal Headquarters in One
L'Enfant Plaza, Washington D.C. They wanted action, and fast. These
bombings were a great distraction and bad press for the Postal Service.
The presidents of the four postal unions were pressuring the Post
Office to ensure the safety of their union members. Postal
management felt the same way, but to that extent, was doing all it
could. It had the Inspection Services around the country on the alert
for copycat bombings. Plus, the FBI was assisting as much as it could.
However, the brunt of the attention was on the St. Paul Inspection
Service. As the head of that agency, Mike White was looked at to
resolve the situation or someone would be sent in to do it for him.
That was pretty much the text of Washington's communication to his
office. Mike had called for a meeting that morning. The meeting
would involve the St. Paul Police Department, the Inspection Service,
and the FBI. When Mike arrived that morning, Fred Cosman was
already there.
"Morning Fred, what brings you here today?"
"I finished up those two arbitration cases you wanted me to close out.
I'm ready to jump back in to help solve those bombing cases."
White paused for a minute, bit his lower lip, and got behind his desk.
"OK. Sit in on the meeting, and we'll try to bring you up to speed."
Unknown to White, Fred had been following the cases. He had been

talking to Inspector Roy plus monitoring inter-office communications. He felt he knew about as much as he could without having access to White's files.

"Anything new since the last bombing? Has the latest forensic file come back from the FBI office?"

Mike looked up, "Why don't we wait till the rest get here. Then we can go over it. I'd rather not have to explain it twice."

"Sure Mike," Fred sat down in the leather couch opposite the desk. The rest of the newly formed task team started to arrive. FBI Agent James was the last to arrive. When he saw Fred, he looked over at White, then he turned his head towards Fred.

"Good to see you again Fred. How ya been?"

"Hi James. Doing good. Did'ya miss me?"

Agent James felt Fred's comment had a slight edge to it. He sat down in a chair near the desk, put his briefcase on the floor, and opened it. "What ya got for us James?" Mike said.

"I think Chief of Police Pat Harrison should go first; he has some new developments." Mike turned to the Police Chief. "Ok then, what ya got for us Pat?"

"A few days ago, one of our uniformed officers stopped a vehicle for a simple traffic violation. There were some college-aged guys in the car. While the officer was checking out the driver's license, he noticed what appeared to be electronic type stuff in the back seat. He asked a few questions, and the driver was really nervous. He went back to check out the license and found out that the driver had an outstanding warrant. He called for backup and arrested the two guys.

Inspector Roy spoke up. "Why did he arrest the passenger?"

"Since the office impounded the car, the passenger had no ride. Besides, he was acting fidgety. The officer took him down to the station under the pretense of giving him a ride. They talked with the driver, a Paul Horning. He was being a real jerk. Saying he knew his rights and all that shit. And get this. He said this shit won't happen when the revolution starts. Well, that really got our attention. Plus, it also gave us a reason to hold the passenger as well. Found out they belonged to Antifa." The Chief took out a folder. "Seems they belong to a local group or some shit like that."

Mike leaned forward, "Think they have any ties to the bombings, Pat?"

"Not sure. The crap they had in the back of their car had all the making for a bomb. But then again, it could end up just being electronic parts."

Fred said, "That's it? It could or could not be bomb material?"

The Police Chief turned around. "And you, who are you?"

Mike White introduced Fred. "This is our lead inspector, Fred Cosman. He just rejoined the team. He was on D dock when it exploded."

"Oh really, hope you weren't hurt."

"No. Just a few scratches."

"Good to hear. But ya, that's all we got, but it's significant."

"How's that?" White got up to get a cup of coffee. "Anybody want some?" No one answered. White leaned against his desk and sipped his coffee.

The Police Chief went on. "Now we know that Antifa is starting to surface with anti-establishment rhetoric. Also, we found two of their members riding around with electronic gadgetry. Plus, this Paul Horning is no student, but a fugitive."

Fred spoke up again. "C'mon that's kind of slim? A kid with a warrant, some electronic gear, plus he supposedly belongs to Antifa. That's a long way from three bombings."

The Police Chief turned. "Fred, Fred Cosman, isn't it?" Fred nodded. "Fred, that's way more than the person who was previously on the case had."

Fred felt the sting of the remark and realized he didn't like this guy. He thought the Chief was a condescending jerk who was impressed with his own rank and position.

White felt the tension. "Look, let's get back on track here. Any other names?" The Chief looked at Fred, then looked at White and put the folder away.

"We have some people of interest, but we're still gathering intel on them."

Inspector Roy brought the team up to speed on the latest bombing findings of the D dock explosions and the other two bombs. FBI Agent James presented some data on the bombing materials. All three bombs were of the same type, same construction. As Fred sat there, he was reminded of James' comment of a bomb signature. After a few hours, the team broke up. White had impressed on them the importance of progress to satisfy Postal Headquarters.

As Fred was walking out, White called him aside.

"What the hell's going on Fred? Why'd ya get into a pissing contest with the Chief for?"

"I wasn't trying to Mike. He's got an attitude, thinks his shit doesn't stink. Big man because he's Chief of Police. He's got a few kids locked up and thinks he's solving the case."

"Fred, look. The Chief is from New York, a big city and maybe he has a big city attitude. But give him his proper's."

"Why?"

"Fred, the Chief is from the old school. When ya get the rank, ya get to name the game. He wasn't always a Chief of Police."

"So?"

"Back in the day, he was a detective with a special terrorist unit team. They were following an Al-Qaeda cell team. They were close to making a big bust when the planes hit the Twin Towers. He was down there when the towers collapsed."

"Ok, well I'll give him that. It was a bad thing. But what's that have to do with Antifa and these two kids?"

"Fred, when I said he was down there, I mean he was there when the first World Trade Tower collapsed. He was in that lobby before it collapsed. If he hadn't been called away, he would have been in there. He lost a couple of buddies in the rubble. I'm afraid he was affected by it. His team might have been close to capturing the plane hijackers before they boarded the planes. Afterwards he transferred out here to get away from the big city thing. And now here he is involved in other bombings, in his city. Guess he may be taking it a bit personal."

"Alright Mike. I can see where he's coming from, but there are three agencies working on this. Ya think he'd share the workload instead of taking it personally."

"Maybe you're right Fred, but let's cooperate with these other agencies. We need all the help we can get."

"Alright Mike, alright, I'll play nice." Fred got his coat and left.

CHAPTER 11

The workload was heavy, and the week went by fast. There were no new leads, but Fred kept going over the bombing reports looking for a common denominator. It was Thanksgiving Day and Fred was the only one in the office. As far as he knew, he was the only one in the building. He came in early and wanted to leave by eleven o'clock. Fred was expected over to his parents' house for Thanksgiving dinner, and he didn't want to be late. Last Sunday's dinner was not pleasant. He and John brokered a truce between them, but barely talked to each other. Fred couldn't wait to leave. Hopefully, today will be different.

He arrived at one in the afternoon and entered the backdoor again through the kitchen.
"Hi Mom."
"Hello Fred, grab yourself a beer out of the fridge and go in the living room. I made your father go to the store for me to pick up a few last-minute items; he should be back before the hour. John's running late, he just called."

Thanksgiving was the only dinner that the Cosmans ate later than usual. After church, the parents would go to Joey's grave and lay down flowers. It would come up during dinner, but there was nothing Fred could do about that.
"Say Fred, could you go down in the basement and get two cans of peas? They're over by your Dad's work bench."
Fred went downstairs and noticed his dad still hadn't gotten rid of that funky smell. He thought it smelled strangely familiar. He grabbed the two cans of peas and went to shut off the basement light when he stepped on a piece of plastic that cracked under his weight. He picked up his foot and looked down. He thought, 'what the hell?" Picking up the pieces, he realized it was the battery back plate of an old-style Nokia cell phone. He turned it over in his hands trying to make sense

of it. His father hated cell phones and Fred was not even sure he had one. He looked over at his father's work bench and saw some wires hidden by a piece of cloth. He went over and took the cloth off, there were thin gauged wires underneath. Fred was a little puzzled, he placed the cloths back.

"Fred! Where are those peas?", his mother yelled from upstairs.

"Coming Mom." Fred shut off the basement light and went the stairs.

"Say Mom, does Dad have a cell phone?"

"Sure, he does. That is, I believe he does. I barely see him use it, who's he going to call?"

"Well, had John been over during the week? I mean aside for Sunday dinners?"

"Why yes. He comes over to check on your father, see if he needs anything. He fixes a few things your father can't or reaches for things up high. Those kinds of things. Why do you ask?"

"Does he do things for Dad in the basement?"

"I suppose. He does whatever needs to be done. Why are you asking all these questions?"

"Oh, just curious I guess."

"Well, you know what they say, curiosity………"

Fred smiled and kissed his mother on the forehead. "Ya Mom, I know, curiosity will kill a cat or something like that." Fred put the peas down, grabbed his beer, and went into the living room and put the TV on.

Shortly, Wentworth Cosman walked in the house followed by John.

"Look who I bumped into on the driveway?" Fred suspected that John had been waiting outside in the driveway because he saw his Volvo. Ol'man Cosman put the small bag of groceries down on the kitchen counter and brushed the snow off his coat.

"Wentworth, what took you so long? I was wondering if you got lost."

"Oh, I ran into Sven over at the Hy-Vee grocery store. We chatted a bit. He wants me to come down to Murphy's. I put him off and said maybe."

"Why I think that would be good for you Wentworth. You should do that."

"Ya, maybe." John and his father went into the living room.

"Hello Fred, when did you get here?"

"About a half hour ago."

"Well, you two gonna say hello? Or is it gonna be like Sunday and you two sit there like mummies? I don't know what's up with you two, but in this house, my house, you're family. You two got that?" Both men nodded. Fred felt that perhaps John was waiting outside after he spotted Fred's Volvo in the driveway and decided to wait for the ol'man to show up in his truck.

The dinner went without a hitch. The mother stayed in the kitchen tidying up. She never went in to watch the Vikings with the men. She felt it important for the boys and their father to have some men time together. It did her heart good to see her boys and her husband together, but it also hurt that Joey was not there. Going to his grave this morning was a combination of relief and grief. She was relieved feeling he was close by. Yet she felt grief because she couldn't hold him anymore or see his smile. She remembered the day he was born. There was a bit of sadness for her knowing that this would be her last child. She wanted to keep him young as long as she could. The other two were growing up so fast, she wasn't ready to let go of their childhood. She dried the last of the dishes and put them in the cupboard.

Ol'man Cosman was asleep in the Lazy Boy chair. The Vikings were minutes away from losing their third straight game.

Fred turned to John. "Mom said you've been coming over to help Dad."

"Is this an investigation?"

"Really John? You going there? You can't have a decent conversation without wise remarks? I just thought it was nice you came over to help him. Makes me feel that I should've been doing the same."

"Look Fred, I know you're involved with this bombing thing and your

office has been poking around asking questions about me. So, let's get
to the point. You have something to ask me, come right out and ask it.
Don't go behind my back!"

"Who's been asking about you?"

"Don't be coy Fred! It's that buddy of yours, Inspector Roy, whatever
his name is. My guys have been coming up to me saying he's asking
about me. Hell, there was a police squad car outside my house a few
nights ago. Tell the ol'man I had to leave." Abruptly, John got his coat
and left. Fred sat there wondering what the hell was going on. Roy
doing an investigation without running it by him. This wasn't good.
White wouldn't go behind his back, he's not the type. They were
supposed to be looking at Antifa or a lone wolf character. Fred didn't
know where to turn, who to trust, Roy, White, James, the Chief, or for
that matter, his own brother John.

CHAPTER 12

Ruth Severson stepped into Matt's Bar ahead of her three roommates. They were celebrating the end of finals and their sophomore fall semester. It was a short, but cold fifteen-minute walk from their University of Minnesota dormitory to the bar. Matt's was on the corner of Cedar Ave S and E 35 St. A large Budweiser sign hung outside the white building. As they entered inside, Ruth spotted a booth against the wall. Perfect! The booth would shield the girls from any draft when the front door to Matt's was opened. They settled in and took off their coats. One of the girls picked up a menu.
"What'da ya gonna have girls?"
Ruth spoke up. "If you don't come for the Jucy Lucy, you shouldn't come at all."

Matt's was known for its great burger, the Jucy Lucy. It got its name when a customer came in and asked for two hamburger patties with a piece of cheese in the middle. When it came, the customer allegedly said, "Now that's a juice lucy" The bar dropped the i, the e, added a y and thus the Jucy Lucy burger was created. After that, Matt's was known as the place of the original Jucy Lucy.

A young slender built guy wearing an apron came over. Ruth looked up and was drawn to the guy's blue eyes. His long hair and unshaven face did not distract from the baby blues. Ruth smiled and put down her menu.
"We'll have four Jucy Lucy's with fries and four cokes."
The waiter wrote their order on a pad and picked up the menus.
"The ladies know what they want. I like that." He winked at Ruth and walked away. The girls giggled.
"Wow Ruth, looks like someone has an admirer."
Ruth smiled. "Get outta here Jan, he's just looking for a good tip."
Her redheaded girlfriend leaned towards Ruth, smiled and spoke. "Oh

no Ruth, he winked at you. What kind of a tip you gonna give him?"
The three girls laughed. Ruth blushed a little. After fifteen minutes,
the blue-eyed waiter came back with their orders.
"Here ya go ladies. Four Jucy Lucy's with fries and four cokes." He
looked at Ruth, "and for you dear lady, I have something special."
Ruth looked up in surprise. She felt a warmth coming over her. Ruth
knew her midwestern winter cheeks were going to blush big time. He
handed her some napkins. The other three girls laughed after the
blue-eyed waiter had left. Ruth felt a bit awkward and embarrassed.
After the girls ate, Ruth picked up the tab to split the cost. She looked
at the bill and looked up quick.
"Ohhhhhhhh!"
The red-haired girl spoke. "What's the matter Ruth, too much?"
Ruth pressed her lips together, with wide eyes and an angry frown she
looked at the girls. "That arrogant SOB put his name and phone
number on the bill!"
One of the other girls took the bill. "It says Wentworth Cosman and
yup, he gave you his phone number."
"What do you mean me? There are four of us!"
The redhead said, "ya but Ruth, he gave you the napkins." The other
two girls laughed as they left Matt's.

The following Saturday Ruth was called down to the front desk of her
resident hall. As she approached the desk, she couldn't believe her
eyes.
"Hi Ruth, how ya been?"
In front of Ruth stood the arrogant blue-eyed SOB from Matt's Bar.
The SOB looked at her and smiled. "Since, I didn't hear from you, I
thought maybe you lost my name and phone number, so I decided to
pay you a cordial visit."

Ruth looked at him and got angry. "What gives you the right to bother
me? How did you find me and how do you know my name?" Ruth
stood there with her hands on her hips. Her unwelcomed suiter

backed up smiling. He had his hands halfway in the air as if in surrender.

"Whoaaaaa, calm down, I came in peace. One question at a time." The SOB kept smiling and Ruth couldn't take her attention off his beautiful blue eyes.

First of all, my name is Wentworth not 'you' and my intent is not to bother you but to get to know you. Second, I overheard your girlfriends call you Ruth at Matt's Bar the night all of you were there. I figured you were a student at the U of M and so I just went through the student directory and here I am."

"What do you mean giving us your phone number? You must think pretty highly of yourself for a waiter." Ruth kept her lips tight, and her eyes frowned.

"Well, technically I intended my phone number to be for you. And yes, I'm a waiter right now. I took a sabbatical from school for the fall semester."

Ruth eyes got wide. "You're a student?"

"Yup, but don't look so surprised. I'm in my senior year at the University of Michigan, Ann Arbor campus. I was studying to be a mechanical engineer. Decided to take some time off and get involved in the peace movement."

"What? Are you one of those radicals with the long hair and beard?" Ruth stood her ground.

The SOB smiled. "Remember, John Adams and Thomas Jefferson were called radicals, plus they had long hair."

"Ya wise guy, so were Karl Marx and Fidel Castro." Ruth paused, "of course, they didn't have long hair. But still the same."

"Touché dear lady, touché."

Ruth relaxed her stance a bit. "And don't call me that. You make me feel like my mother."

"Ok Ruth, I won't call you a lady."

"Now you trying to be smart?"

Wentworth spoke softly and smiled. "No Ruth, I'm just trying to get to know you. That's all."

Ruth's composure was very relaxed now and she fidgeted a little. She looked down and then up at those blue eyes.

"Why?"

"Because I liked you the minute I saw you walk in. You had a nice face. Hell, you weren't even my table. I made my friend switch with me."

Ruth felt the flush starting in her cheeks and turned away. She had to admit to herself she was flattered. Here was this guy who traded his workstation to wait on her and he took the time to find out where she was. To her, that had to count for something.

"So, what now Wentworth?"

"I have something for you." Ruth didn't know what to say. Wentworth reached in his pocket and pulled out a handful of napkins and handed them to her.

Ruth had to contain a big smile and just gave a smirk. She took the napkins. "Think you're pretty smart, huh?"

"Well girl, a person can't have too many napkins. Besides that's all I can afford for now."

"What do you mean for now? You think I'm going to let some guy in my life because of napkins?"

Wentworth just smiled. "No Ruth, it's just something to break the ice."

Ruth found herself liking this guy. He was unconventional, original, and he did make an effort to find her. Besides, he really did seem nice and sometimes a girl had to trust her instincts.

Ruth spoke. "I better get back upstairs. It's getting to be nine and they frown on guys being here late."

"Sooo Ruth, you mind if I call you?"

Ruth smiled as she started to turn away. "Maybe."

She watched him almost skip out of the building as he left. Maybe this is something she thought.

A week went by, and Ruth and Wentworth went out. Most times were walks around Lake Harriet. Even with snow on the ground, it was a beautiful walk. They walked by grand houses and marveled at them. Sometimes they stopped in at the Turtle Bread Company, a small coffee shop, and shared a deli sandwich. During this time, Wentworth disappeared for days without calling her. When she asked him where he was, it was always some meeting he had to attend. Since Ruth wasn't political, she didn't push it, until one day she got a call. Wentworth was in jail and asked if she'd come down and get him out. "How come you were in jail? What's this all about Wentworth?" "Look Ruth, a bunch of us were protesting over at the Minneapolis Capitol. Well things got a little pushy and the cops arrested us." "What did you guys do that caused you to be arrested? They don't arrest people just for protesting." Ruth waited for an answer. "Sometimes these things get a little heated. There was a large crowd, people pushed forward. Some jerks threw a bottle at the cops and that's all it took. The cops said they were assaulted and started dragging people away. They weren't being polite either. I got caught up in the mayhem and that's that."

Ruth didn't know what to say and let the matter drop. Over the course of her spring semester, she saw less of Wentworth. He was either on a ride to protest in Washington DC or in Chicago protesting. She was sure he had been arrested more than he let on. He always made it a point to call her no matter where he was. When he was in Minneapolis, he spent all his time with her. In her junior fall semester, Wentworth enrolled back at the Ann Arbor Campus to complete his degree in mechanical engineering. It was during this period that bombings were taking place. Police stations and any military recruiting office were targets. Even some college campuses where the military had contracts were bombed. Ruth was concerned for Wentworth because the Ann Arbor campus was a center of radical protestors. The Weathermen Underground was formed on that campus. Ruth was never sure if Wentworth was involved. All she knew was that when he was with her, he was the sweetest person and he never spoke about the protests. In March of 1970, there was a bomb blast in a basement apartment in Greenwich Village. The building was partially destroyed, and three Weatherman members were killed. In the rubble, the police found fifty-seven sticks of dynamite, four completed bombs, six detonators, and other bombing material. Ruth was sickened. She felt somehow that Wentworth was involved and was possibly one of those killed. For the rest of the semester, she didn't hear from him. No calls or letters. Her worst fears haunted her.

Ruth graduated with honors from the University of Minnesota on a beautiful sunny day. She went up on the stage to receive her diploma. As she was walking down the steps, she looked at the back of the crowd and almost fainted. Ruth grabbed the handrail to steady herself. As she looked back, she saw the most beautiful blue eyes and smile. She hurried down the stairs and with tears in her eyes ran to him.

"Wentworth! Wentworth!" She reached out to him and hugged him tight. She felt his warmth, his strength, and his scent. For a short moment, the world stopped for Ruth. Then in a moment she froze, looked up at him and anger shadowed in her face. She started to hit him in the chest with her small hands.

"Where the hell have you been? What didn't you call me? I've been worried sick, I thought you might be dead. You jerk!"

"Jerk?" He smiled and chuckled. "Wait a minute. Is that a way to greet me?" He kept smiling as he held her arms.

"I make all this effort to see you graduate and I get called a jerk?" She looked up at his face and realized he had shaven. There was no beard, and his hair was cut nicely, she wondered how she recognized him. But Ruth knew, it was the blues and smile. The months he was gone evaporated. He was here now, alive.

Wentworth spoke. "Hey Ruth, I got you a gift." Wentworth put his hand in his pocket and pulled out a pack of napkins."

Ruth looked down at the napkins, then looked up at him. She started to cry and smile at the same time.

"Whoaaaa girl, they're not that bad." Wentworth smiled. "Hey, they

may not be from Matt's, but they're good to wipe your eyes."
Ruth looked up with teary eyes, took the package with her left hand
and hit him in the chest with her right hand.
"Smart ass!"

Over the next few weeks, they again walked Harriet Lake and had
coffee at the Turtle Bread Company. Days after her graduation, he told
her he couldn't tell her where he had been, and he asked her not to
ask. He said it was for the better and to respect his wishes. Although
Ruth felt hurt, she realized that she had to get by this. So, she did just
that, forgot about it.

Things were good for Ruth and Wentworth. They hung around an area
close to the University of Minnesota, a place called Dinkytown. It was
an area of student life, containing a mix of old bookstores, bike shops,
old clothing stores, and coffee shops. Dinkytown was known for street
musicians that entertained those on a limited budget like Ruth and
Wentworth. They went to anything affordable for a young couple with
little money. After a year of being together, both felt things were
serious between them. They were standing outside the Varsity
Theater on Fourth Street one Friday night. Ruth was searching for a
napkin in her pocket. Wentworth asked what she was doing. Ruth
said she still had some popcorn butter on her small finger. He reached
in his pocket, took out a napkin, and handed it to her. She looked at it
and her eyes started to tear. On the napkin from Matt's Burger place
was a message, 'will you marry me'?
Wentworth smiled, "They still have the best napkins." They were
married later that month.

CHAPTER 13

Fred sat at the end of the bar at the VFW Post 292. He was nursing his second Brandy Manhattan. He rubbed his forehead as he swirled the swizzle stick in his glass. It had been a long day and he decided to leave work early. Fred had spent the entire day going over the FBI bomb forensic files, the St. Paul police report, and the Postal Inspector's reports. The data was roaming around in his head, and he needed to reset his mind. The FBI report gave details about the bomb type indicating it was created by an amateur. The cell phone used to trigger the bomb had no fingerprints on the shattered parts. Aside from the time and dates of the explosions, there was not a lot to go on. The police reports mentioned four names of people of interest. Three names were the college-aged guys who were members of Antifa. They had been arrested for a traffic violation, but had electronic parts, wire, and tape in their car. Their suspicious nature led the police to arrest them. All three lawyered up at the start of their questioning. The fourth name was redacted by a large black line over the name. The Inspector's report contained information gleaned from Inspector Roy Downings and Chuck Yantz, information that Fred had no knowledge of. He also thought it was strange that the Inspectors report was kept in his bosses, Mike White's, office. Since his secretary Allie also did the filing for Mike, Fred talked Allie into getting a copy of the file under penalty of, 'I'll cut your nuts off if you say how you got it'. Allie had no desire to get caught up in office politics. Fred just couldn't understand why he wasn't privy to the information Roy and Chuck had compiled. After all, he was the lead inspector on the case. The file information proved too much for one sitting so Fred had to break away. He was also hoping to run into his brother John at the VFW. He thought they could mend fences and at least get back to some semblance of normalcy. He didn't want to go through another family dinner like Thanksgiving. Fred was staring down at his drink, trying to process everything.

"Buy me a drink sailor?"

"Huh?" Fred knew the voice, but it didn't connect.

"You've been playing with your drink for a while now." He looked into the eyes of Allie.

"Oh, hey Allie. What brings you into this place?"

"We girls," Allie motioned over to three women sitting at a table, "have a lady's night out a few times a month. You know, trash our bosses and complain about the lack of available men."

"You don't actually trash talk me, do you?" Fred wasn't sure he wanted to hear the answer.

"Well, I wouldn't tell you if I did or not," Allie smiled. Actually, my girlfriends think I'm lucky to work for you. They also think you're cute." Fred's interest perked up.

"Really?" Fred smiled and looked over at the women. "What about you, you think I'm cute?"

Allie smiled, "I'll hold my opinion. So, what brings you in here? You never struck me as the type to drink during the week."

"Ahh, this damn bombing case is driving me batty. There is something missing, something just out of reach. I have a sense for something but, I'm unable right now to piece it all together."

"Did that file help at all?"

"It kinda made it worse, there's information in it I wasn't aware off."

"Well, let me know if you need me to steal anything else." Allie started to leave.

"Wait! Do you have to go? Can't ya stay a while? I could use the company."

"As tempting as it sounds, we both know that's not a good idea. Besides my girlfriends might start to gossip and you know how word spreads in the post office."

"Yeah, faster than the internet. Maybe another time?"

"Can't say I would, Fred. Can't say I wouldn't." Allie smiled, turned, and walked back to her table.

Fred thought, that's a fine-looking woman. "Damn PO and it's gossip mill."

"Want another round pal?"

Mike looked up at the bartender. "No Max, I think I've had enough."

Fred decided to go back to work and take another crack at the files. He was about to turn into the post office parking lot when he spotted John's truck parked outside the loading dock gate. He was thinking .... what the hell is John doing there? Fred pulled over and watched. Within ten minutes, John's lights came on and his truck pulled out into traffic. He almost thought of following him but decided against it. He really didn't want to know what John was doing. Fred had to find out who the redacted name in the inspectors' file is.

He decided he had enough of the PO for one day and turned his Volvo around and headed home. When he got to his condo on West Grant Street in Minneapolis, there was a car parked under the building in his guest parking space. As his vehicle pulled into his spot, the headlights shone on Allie leaning up against her car smoking a cigarette. He thought, what the hell is this all about? He got out of his car.

"Hi sailor, got a drink?"

"Allie......what are you doing here?"

"Well, the girls decided to call it an early night. I wasn't tired and remembered you did mention another time."

Fred was a little perplexed. "Ahhh, ya, but I thought another time like later in the future. A week, maybe two weeks."

"Ok, I can go." She dropped her cigarette and squashed it with her foot.

"No, no wait! We're good! Do you want to go back to the Pub? I do have stuff upstairs."

"Look Fred, my car is cold and so am I. I'm not driving back to the Pub. Can we go upstairs?"

On the way towards the elevator Fred asked. "I didn't know you smoked."

"I always smoke when I'm nervous. I had a couple of drinks with the girls and felt bold. But now I feel a bit foolish." Allie kept walking straight without turning around. Fred stopped dead in his tracks with his mouth slightly opened and his eyes wide. He scurried to catch up with Allie. In the elevator, the scent of her perfume inflamed his senses. He thought, oh Lord, I may be out of my league. They walked into the eighth-floor condo, Fred went over, picked up the remote for the fireplace, and watched the flame come on. When he turned around, Allie was already taking off her coat.

"Here let me take that." He went to the entrance closet and got a wooden hanger and hung her coat up. When he turned around, Allie was over by the sliding glass doors looking out over the city.

"Great view. How long have you lived here?"

He walked over and stood slightly behind her and looked out over the city. "I moved in shortly after my divorce. A friend of mine was moving out and told me about the place. It's a bit pricey, but I didn't want to spend time looking around for places, so I thought, what the hell." She turned around, faced him and looked in his eyes. Fred stiffened up, not sure what he should do. Allie smiled.

"You said something about a drink?"

Fred came out of his deer in the headlight look. "Mmmm, yes..., yes! Ahh...come over to the bar my lady, and I shall fix you a drink of your choice." Fred bent slightly at the waist and made a sweeping gesture with his arm from the glass doors towards the bar. He got behind the small wet bar.

"What's your pleasure?"

"Vodka tonic, twist of lemon." Fred got busy making her drink. "So, tell me Mr. Inspector, how long have you been divorced?"

Fred stopped what he was doing, looked up and smiled slightly.

"Oh, so what? Now we're being serious?"

"No, it's just that I've worked for you for a while and know so little about you. You come in, say good morning, exchange pleasantries, and go about your work. During the day I make coffee, bring you files.

At the end of the day, I say goodnight, you say goodnight, and that's it. You're very cordial, respectful...and at times a bit flirtatious like most guys. Yet, I know more about your boss, Mike White, than I do about you. You're pretty closed mouth about your personal life. I knew you were divorced, but not once did you ever mention your wife's name. Hell, I don't even know if you have kids." Allie just looked at him. Fred put Allie's drink on the counter, then put two ice cubes in a glass jigger, and poured some Jameson Whiskey. He swirled the liquid, listening to the ice cubes protesting.

"Well, Kathy and I met in college. Seemed to be a good match to me, anyways that's what I thought. She was from an old Republican Boston family. They were pretty nice people, but I think her staying out here bothered them.

"Fred, I'm sorry I didn't mean to pry. You don't have to go on."

"No, no, actually it's ok to talk about it. I graduated from the University, got promoted to the Inspection service. Things seemed to be going well as far as I thought. Unfortunately, she had a few miscarriages. I think that hit her awfully hard. I was working late many nights trying to prove myself. She was alone too much of the time, and I guess it worked on her. We kinda drifted apart. I did not see it coming. I think back now and see that a young couple should be together. No job should be the cause of a breakup in a marriage. I could've been a better husband, I could've tried harder. Anyway, she went back to Boston, and me... well you know the rest. Allie stared at Fred while he talked, she hadn't touched her drink.

"Oh, Fred I'm sorry. I didn't expect that. I thought it may have been the usual finance thing or drifting apart. Maybe I should go."

"Wait a minute Allie, I just opened myself to you. I thought that was what women liked men to do once in a while instead of keeping it in.

"Yes, but I feel like I pressured you."

Fred lowered his head slightly, did a small chuckle and smiled. "No Allie, it was actually good to hear it out. If I had said all that and there was no one here, then I would need help. Sometimes it's good to vent, and for over a year I've had no one to vent to. Not even my family. I just can't do it."

Allie looked at Fred.... he looked at her. He walked around the end of the small wet bar and kissed her. The soft wetness of her lips was intoxicating to him. Fred led her over to the fireplace. He took two throw pillows off the couch and laid them on the floor.

Fred woke up feeling exhausted but disoriented. The sun came through the blinds. Opening first one eye then the other, he looked over at an empty pillow. He hadn't really drunk much last night, but he felt like he had.

"Allie?......Allie!" No response. He got up and sat at the edge of his couch, rubbed his forehead, and looked at his leg. He had his clothes on. Did I dream it? He went out to the kitchen to make coffee......it was on. Beside the Mr. Coffee was a note.

'Morning sailor. Hope you slept well; must admit you can hurt a girl's feeling falling asleep that fast. I went into your bathroom and when I came out you were asleep. So, I set the coffee timer and left a note, 'see ya tomorrow in the office'.

Shaking his head, Fred thought he was out of practice and made an ass out of himself. Could a person get that tired that he'd fall asleep before having sex without drinking? He got up, took his clothes off, and hit the shower.

CHAPTER 14

Fred got off the elevator and walked to his office door. He hesitated before opening the door, thinking this is gonna be awkward. He walked into the reception area. Allie looked up and said, "Morning sailor." Fred turned and smiled.

"Where're you getting this sailor thing from? That's about the fourth time you called me that."

Allie put her pen down and in a shy manner said, "I got it from an old 50's movie I watched last week. I thought it was cute, but now it sounds kinda stupid. Fred nodded and turned to walk into his inner office. "You want some coffee soldier?"

He stopped, smiled, and shook his head, she got me he thought. He was taking his coat off when Allie walked in.

"By the way, Office Max dropped off the flip chart and the pin-up board."

Fred saw both over in the corner. "Ah ha." He went over and moved the flip chart and board closer to his desk.

"If you don't mind me asking, what're ya gonna do with that stuff?"

"Well, I keep running the facts of the bombings around in my head. It's all jumbled up. I need to write it down, step back, and look at it from a distance. That way I can rearrange facts and make some sense or timeline out of it. We used to do that at the Academy."

She shrugged her shoulders, "whatever." Allie started to leave.

"Ah, Allie, about last night I'm, wel........."

"Don't worry about it. We had both been drinking, besides nothing happened."

"I know, but I just don't want it to make things awkward."

"No, just chalk it up to another of your bombings." She smiled and walked away.

"Ouch!" Fred didn't see that coming.

He had the files open on his desk. The flip chart already had several pieces of information written on the paper. He had created a line in the middle of the chart from top to bottom. This he labeled bombings. Like the trunk of a tree, this was the main or central concept. Going up the trunk, he made branches of information and labeled them. One would be the location of the bombings, another would be the times, another dates. Near the middle, he had the names of the college-aged guys, their association with Antifa, and the FBI forensic report. He included on one branch a large question mark for the unknown name in the reports. He continued this method adding some information, rearranging other data to make better sense of it. Occasionally, he'd step back, look at his findings, and make corrections. He looked at the Antifa guys on the board. Nothing in the Chief's report mentioned where they were the night of the bombings. Also, if they did the bombings, where did they get the material? He wrote that down so he could ask the Chief. That information could be in another file or just not asked. There might be another file he didn't have. Fred looked at the question mark, got a frown on his face, and went to the report of Inspector Downing and Yantz. After the blacked-out name it read, 'along with possible relative, active or retired'. What the hell does that mean, he thought.

It was slightly past one in the afternoon, Fred decided to go down to the in-house cafeteria and get a sandwich. Sitting at his table, he saw Roy Downing walk in with his brown bag lunch. Fred motioned him over. Roy seemed like he was going to leave but went over and sat down.
"You brown bagging it Roy?"
"Ya, the wife has me on a strict regimen. Says I need to lose fifteen pounds." Roy patted his gut. "You know what they say Fred, guys who lose weight live longer than guys who mention that their wives should lose weight."
Fred chuckled and said, "There's some truth in that. Say, where you been Roy? Haven't seen you around for a while, haven't seen Chuck

Yantz either."

"Oh, White has Chuck and I hunting down small leads on those bombings while you look at the big picture."

Fred seemed surprised. "Really? Mike didn't mention anything about that to me."

"Maybe it slipped his mind." Roy kept eating his sandwich without looking up.

"Perhaps I should ask him." Fred was staring at Roy. "What the hell is going on Roy? You and Chuck are out hunting down leads without my knowing it. You two, plus the Chief of Police, the FBI, and White have a meeting without my knowledge, while I'm finishing up some damn arbitration case. And while I'm at it, in your report there is a blacked-out name with the wording, 'along with possible relative, active or retired'. What does that mean?"

Roy seemed a bit nervous. He put down his food and folded his hands in front of him. "Fred, you brought me into the St. Paul Inspectors Branch, helped me out finding my way around. I'm beholding to ya."

"Where's this going Roy? Looks like you're beating around the bush."

"I didn't, that is, me and Chuck didn't cross out no names. We just put down what we found and that was about it. We gave the file to Mike White. As far as the meeting, I wasn't aware you didn't know about it until now."

"Roy! Be straight up with me, whose name is blacked out in the files?"

Gathering his stuff together, Roy stood up and looked at Fred. "It's your brother John."

"My brother? Why the hell do they think he's involved?"

"Think about it Fred. John has been making waves, calling management murderers, said whoever did the bombings should get a medal. Every chance he gets, he's in management's face. Wouldn't you write his name down?"

"Wait a minute! The relative mentioned, is that me?"

"Don't know Fred, I didn't add that part."

"Well, maybe I'll ask Mike White."

"Ya can't."

"And why not?"

"Cause he's in Washington, DC answering questions about the bombings. They're squeezing his nuts pretty good about this thing. Won't be back till tomorrow. Look Fred, Mike has a lot of confidence in ya. If he mentioned a relative in the report, he's just exploring possible scenarios. Spit balling if you will, it's nothing personal. Hell, he mentioned one time that when he retires, he hopes you get to replace him. Now does that sound like a guy who doesn't trust you?"

"Well Roy that may have been before the bombings. I got to speak to the Chief tomorrow, I've got some questions for him."

"Better you than me Fred. That man's too intense. Take care guy."

"Take it easy Roy." Fred pushed his plate away. After the Chief, he wanted to speak to the Antifa guys, maybe even Mike when he comes back. Between the three of them lies the answer. He got up and went back to his office to work on the chart.

It was dark outside now; Allie had left an hour ago. Fred was slumped down in his chair, the sleeves to his shirt were rolled up and his tie pulled slightly down. He felt emotionally exhausted. The flip chart, and pin-up board were full of writing. There was something there, but it wasn't jumping out. He had been going at it straight for five hours. Fred thought about what Roy had said. He got up, walked over to the flip chart, and put a circle around John's name, the Antifa guys, and the FBI forensic file. These were the knowns. If he could eliminate the knowns, the underlying cause would surface. His cell phone rang, and he picked it up.

"FRED! Oh Fred!" A hysterical women's voice was on the other end, it was his mother.

"Mom, what's wrong?"

"Fred, you have to get over here right now! Please? I don't know what to do."

"What's the matter? Is it Dad? Something happen?"

"Oh Fred, John came over to see your father. He went downstairs to the basement. All of a sudden, I heard shouting. Your father and John were shouting at each other. I've never seen Wentworth like that, or John either. Then John started throwing stuff around, shouting, and he knocked a bench over. Then he came upstairs and stormed out of the house. I went down to see if your father was alright. He was angry and wouldn't say anything. He grabbed his coat and said this would not have happened if Joey was still alive, then he left the house. I think he may be going down to Murphy's. Oh Fred, please come over, I don't know what to do."

"Alright Mom, alright. I'm leaving now, try to calm down, I'll be there in a little bit."

Fred parked his Volvo and went into the house through the kitchen door. His mother was sitting at the kitchen table, her legs crossed at the ankles, and she was wringing her hands.

"Mom!" Ruth got up and gave him a long hug and then separated. He held her arms with his hands. "What the heck is going on?" She was sobbing slightly, dabbed her eyes with the hanky she kept in her apron pocket.

"Oh Fred. It was terrible, I never saw them like that. First it was quiet, and then I heard them shouting at each other, then something crashed. I went downstairs and they were at each other. I didn't know what to do."

"Ok Mom, ok. I'm gonna go downstairs and look around." His mother sat back down, dabbed at her eyes, and crossed her ankles again. The basement was a mess, Fred made his way slowly through the carnage. He went over to where the work bench was and saw wires, pieces of cell phones, and some other parts he didn't recognize. On the floor was a manilla folder with newspaper clippings sticking out. He picked the folder up and started to go through the clippings. He didn't know what to make of it. Fred put the folder under his arm, looked around, and went back upstairs.

"What did you find? Anything to help explain their yelling?"

He took the folder and opened it. "Mom' have you ever seen this before?"

"What is it?"

"A collection of clippings from the seventies. Things about a bombing in New York, articles about protests, things like that."

His mother got quiet and put her head down. She kept wringing the hanky in her hands.

"Mom, do you know anything about these clippings?"

"No, I never saw them before."

"O... kay, you never saw them before, but do you know anything about them?"

"Not really. You see back in the day when I first met your father, it was a tense period. The Vietnam War protests were going on all over the country. College students were protesting in the streets, police were pushing back. There was the Kent State shooting where the Ohio National Guard killed some students. A group called the Students for a Democratic Society was formed. A splinter group was created, The Weather Underground. They did some bombings. Your father was kinda a member."

"Mom? What'da ya mean he was kinda a member, was he a member or not?"

She wrung the hanky a bit more. "I don't know Fred, he knew them, went to protests, but your father would never do anything like that."

Fred was astonished. He held the folder in his hand and slowly sat down. "Dad was a protester? Heck' I didn't even know he went to college. So, were these his clippings?"

"Yes, maybe, oh I don't know, I never saw those clippings."

"Mom, how often did John come over?"

"Oh, maybe two times a week."

"Was Dad here when John came over?"

"Sometimes, other times John just went into the basement and worked down there, cleaning up and such, I guess."

"Well, there are two people who know the owner of these clippings. Mom, do you mind if I take these clippings?"

"No, no, just get them out of the house."

"I'm gonna go find John and Dad. There's only a few places they would go to." Fred kissed his mother on the forehead and left.

The first place he went to was Murphy's Bar and Grill. He walked in and there were only a few people there. The next place was the VFW Post 292. He asked Max the bartender if he saw John or his Dad. Max hadn't seen either of them. Fred drove to John's house; the place was dark, no one answered the door. He next went to the post office loading area; he didn't see John's truck or his father's. Fred sat in his car thinking; they have to show up somewhere. It was ten thirty and he was chasing ghosts. He decided to call it a night and go. I'll have to follow this up tomorrow he thought. He pulled out into the traffic and went home.

CHAPTER 15

Fred got into his office at nine thirty. He had called his mother earlier. She said his dad came home late, didn't say anything, and went to bed. He got up early this morning and left the house. Fred called John, got his message machine so he left a message. He grabbed a cup of coffee to go and headed out the door. When he got to his office, Allie was doing some filing.

"Morning Fred. Wow, you look like hell, bad night?"

"Yes, barely slept at all. Can you get me the St. Paul's Chief of Police's number?" Allie came back with the number and went back to the filing. Fred called the Chief.

"Hello?"

"Morning Chief, this is Fred Cosman. I've been going over the files on the bombings. I laid out a kind of time frame and picture board. I'm wondering if the Antifa guys had an alibi for the times of the bombing, and did we ever connect them with a source of bomb making material. I didn't see anything regarding that in the files."

"Ya, that's partially my fault. I kept a small written account of things I asked them but forgot to put them in the files. They're clean on the alibis, all three were in jail on rioting charges at the time. That's why one of them had an outstanding warrant. He failed to appear in court, the other two showed up."

"What about where they obtained material to make a bomb?"

"Strange thing about that. I had a note to call you. We're gonna have to release these guys."

"Release them! Why?"

"During my interrogations, one of the guys mentioned that they were getting material for some older guy. This old guy asked for material in pieces, not at the same time. Since the purchases were spread out, these guys weren't suspicious. Besides, the older guy paid good."

Fred got a sickening feeling in his stomach. "You said it was an older guy? How old?"

"Hell, these Antifa guys are in their early twenties. Anybody over thirty is old to them. There used to be a saying, 'don't trust anybody over thirty'. I guess there is an exception if they pay good. This older guy could be anyone over thirty."

"That's it? Anything else."

"No, we're looking at a couple of leads. But for now, the Antifa guys seemed to be off our list. That FBI guy James agrees with me."

"Hell, this kinda puts everything back at square one."

"For now, Fred, but things will turn up, they always do."

Fred's mind was swirling, his main suspects were considered non-players by the Chief and the FBI. His only possible leads pointed right at his family. He needed to talk with John and his dad. He went back to his office to attack the flip chart and rearrange the data.

Allie was typing away on the computer.

"How did it go with the Chief?"

"Seems like when I get on a hot trail, it evaporates. People of interest are no longer people of interest."

"Oh, your brother called a while back. Said he'd get back to you." Fred went into his office and called John.

"Hello?"

"John! Where the hell have you been? We got to talk guy. Mom's totally upset about you and Dad. What the hell is going on?"

"Fred, things aren't what they seem. I've been following Dad, he's all over the place."

"What are you talking about? Both you and Dad have some explaining to do. What do you know about the paper clipping's I found in Dad's basement?"

"That's just part of it, Fred. It also involves Joey's death. There's a lot we didn't know about. Meet me down at Murphy's in an hour."

"What's Joey's death got to do with this? Hello? Hello?" The phone was dead. Fred put his phone down on his desk. Oh crap, what the hell is happening here. Allie walked in.

"Say Fred I have to......what's wrong with you? You look like you've been hit in the gut."

"Ahh, I feel like it. Stuff is happening and it's hard to process. What were you gonna say?"

"I have that dentist appointment I mentioned last week so I'm heading out now."

"Ya, Ok."

'You sure you don't want me to hang around? Anything I can help you with?"

"No, I gotta work this out. I am heading out to meet someone, I may not be back."

Allie left the office. Fred grabbed his coat and walked to the elevator. Before he pressed the button, he decided to see Mike White. Fred entered White's office and walked right by the receptionist.

"We gotta talk guy." Mike White was in the process of filling a cardboard box.

"Hello Fred. I meant to call you." Fred stopped and looked at Mike and the desk.

"What the hell's going on? What're ya doing?"

"I'm moving on out. Decided to take an early retirement, with the blessings of headquarters." Fred was dumfounded.

"What'da ya mean retirement? Why? What the hell is going on?"

"Well, the powers that be figured that maybe I overextended my time here. Basically, they're not happy with my handlings of these bombings. The optics don't look so good in the press. They think I lost my touch; want to bring in a special counsel to oversee things. I told them that's fine, but I wouldn't be there. Imagine that, a bunch of bureaucrats telling me I needed help. Hell, I was working on the Unabomber case while they were still in grade school. I don't need this shit; I've got my time in and plenty more."

"But cha' can't leave now. Who's gonna coordinate things between the FBI, the Chief, Roy, Chuck, and the bombing reports?"

White put a small picture and a medallion in the box. He looked up and smiled. "I suggested they put you in charge. You're young but you're good."

"Me? For Christ sake Mike, are you outta ya mind? I can't handle the stuff you do."

"Yes, you can Fred, ya just don't want to. You have what it takes to do the job, but you're more comfortable flying under the wire, investigating, and sending your reports to me. Very detailed reports. You're good at this job. Besides, Roy and Chuck think highly of you, that's good leadership by example. Time for you to cross that line, take charge. By the way, what was it you came in here for?"

Fred was almost in a trance processing Mike's word, but all he heard in his head was blah, blah, blah, until the last question. He heard himself repeat it, "Come in here for? Oh, ya, I had some concerns about what was in the bombing reports."

"Like what?"

There was a statement that listed my brother John as a person of interest."

"C'mon Fred, he was making comments that are hard to overlook. You must've realized that?"

Fred looked at him. "It was the following sentence that said, 'or relatives active or retired'. That's a clear reference to me. Am I considered a 'person of interest'?"

"Of course not. But Fred, I have to entertain all possibilities even if they're a stretch of the imagination. For me not to do so would be negligent. Hell, you've done the same thing if you were in my place. Both Agent James and the Chief had the same thoughts. Ya gotta throw stuff out there and see what sticks to the wall. You know yourself; you eliminate the knowns and what's left is the cause. You're overthinking this thing." White threw some more personal items in the box and paused. "Well, I guess I'll finish up tomorrow."

Fred looked at his watch. "Oh shit, I'm supposed to meet someone right now. I'll catch ya tomorrow Mike." Fred bolted out of Mike White's office and made a beeline for Murphy's.

The bar had a few regular customers, some would call them bar flies. Over in the corner was John. He sat there looking down at his hands wrapped around a glass of beer. Fred looked at the clock on the wall as he walked over, only ten minutes late, 'good he thought'.
"Hi John."
His brother looked up, smiled slightly, and looked back down at his beer. "You weren't in much of a rush, were you?"
"Sorry, last-minute conversation with the boss."
"How's the ol' SOB doing? Still busting the Union's balls?"
"C'mon John. Mike's not like that. He's a straight shooter."
"Straight shooter my ass, he hates the Unions, just like you."
Fred got a little tense. "That's not true John and you know it. I'm Ok with Unions, it's Union management I don't care for. Just like upper postal management, they're out for themselves. They don't give a rip about the rank and file. Most union leaders come up through the ranks. They only know one way of doing things, same goes for postal management. They do what they've always done before. Occasionally a newbie comes along with outside management experience, and he gets buried in the 'postal way' of doing things. I could give you plenty of examples, but that's not what I'm here for. Now what the hell is going on with you and Dad?"
"Dad?" John huffed. "Our shining Dad, our solid Dad, our idol. He always preached to us about right and wrong. That it's never too late to do the right thing. To me, he was the most solid, easiest going guy I knew. But ever since Joey was killed, he hasn't been the same. All this time I was blaming the post office for his death. I thought they murdered Joey because of faulty safety conditions. Ya, I felt the same way as Dad until the other day. He turned to Fred. Ya know that guy Sparks? The tall guy that worked with Joey on the docks?"
Fred realized John had had too many beers. "Sure, he and Joey worked together all the time."
"Well, while all this shit is piling up, the FBI, the police, and your office buddies are coming around asking questions. The other night after a

union meeting, Sparks comes up to me. He's real edgy ya know. Said he was getting nervous about the bombings and thought he might somehow be implicated, be involved."

Fred sat back. "Get involved, how?"

"That's what I said, how? Sparks says he thinks they may be trying to tie in Joey's death with the bombings."

"What the hell does Joey's death got to do with the bombings?"

"Think of it Fred. All the bombings started shortly after Joey died. Oh, excuse me, after Joey's 'industrial accident'."

Fred overlooked the slight jab at management.

"John! John, I'm not following your logic, and what has this to do with you and Dad?"

"I'm coming to that. John took another sip of beer. "Sparks told me that he was there the night Joey died. Said he saw Joey's hair get caught in the conveyer belt. Saw him get slammed into the gears."

"John, this is not helping me understand..."

"Hold on, hold on." John pushed his beer away from him. "Sparks said it was Joey who removed the chain guards from the conveyor belts."

"Joey?"

"Ya, Joey. He said Joey had been doing it for a couple of days. It made the conveyor go into the truck, closer to the mail bags. That way they could unload the mail trucks faster. Then Joey could go home on time and work on the house he had bought for him and his future bride. Imagine that, for a stupid house he got killed."

Fred was dumbfounded. "Why the hell didn't Sparks say something?"

"Hell, for a lot of reasons. I was the main one. I made such a big deal out of postal management safety policies that Sparks didn't know what to do. Does he go against his own union? If he says anything, does he betray Joey? The guy was confused. He thought if he didn't say anything, it would all go away. So, there you have it. Joey caused his own death."

"John, that doesn't explain why you and Dad went at each other. Did ya tell Dad? Is that why you guys got into an argument?"

"No, no, I never got the chance. Look Fred, I've been going over to Dad's since Joey's death. Helping him out, lend an ear …. whatever! But I started to notice a few things down in the basement. Wires on the work bench, tape, old cell phone parts, that kinda shit."

"So, what did you make of it? Seems harmless enough to me."

"You would think so wouldn't ya? But in one of the workbench drawers there was a drawing of postal docks." John looked up at Fred. "Ya, postal docks. I really didn't think much about it. Although I thought it was weird. But Dad did work on the docks, right? So, I thought maybe he was remembering where he had worked. John shook his head. "I don't know."

"John! Focus, what caused you to trash Dad's basement?"

"Fred, there was a folder of old bombings clippings from the sixties, I looked them over and thought 'Oh no'. Well, Dad came home and quickly came down to the basement. I asked him about the folder, the wires, and the cellphone parts. He blew up. Said I had no right being in his basement. I lost it! I looked him in the face and asked if he knew anything about the bombings. I didn't know why I said that, but I did. Damn, if he didn't look me straight in the face and said, YES! God damn it yes, I 'm partially responsible. Said he should've gone to the authorities He kept yelling that they, the post office, had murdered his Joey. That they took away the last chapter of his life. Dad reached out his arm and swiped everything off the work bench, sent things flying everywhere. You should've seen his eyes, Fred. He yelled at me; THEY KILLED MY SON! THEY KILLED MY JOEY! We screamed and yelled, no one won.' It was a losing argument, I stormed out."

Fred was confused as to what to do now. He had a dad possibly involved in a bombing, a brother who could be listed as an accomplice, and I'm the one investigating the case. Sarcastically, he thought 'oh ya, no one could have a problem with this'.

Fred turned to his brother. "John, was Dad left-handed?"

"I don't know. What the hell kinda question is that?"

"Did'ja tell anybody else about this thing with Dad?"

John looked up in surprise. "Told this to who? Hell, Fred it just happened yesterday. I didn't have time to see or tell anybody. Nor would I've told anyone, 'cause I don't know what to do." John's shoulder slumped as if the life just left his body. He was looking down at the table. "Christ Fred, how did our family become so dysfunctional so fast? I know what I should do." John looked back up at Fred. "But if Dad's involved, I can't be the one that turns him in." He looked at his brother with pleading eyes.

Fred leaned back in his chair, he felt emotionally exhausted. He knew what John had just asked. Their father fit the FBI's description of the alleged bomber, left-handed, amateur bomb maker, and a knowledge of dock operations. It was Fred's investigation and he had to go wherever the information led him. That information brought him right to his family's own front door. It was then that Fred's cell phone rang, he looked at it and saw it was Roy Downing.
"Hello?"
"Fred this is Roy. Ya have to come down to the St. Paul Post Office docks fast, I think we got our bomber trapped." Chuck's here and Mike White. FBI agent James is on the way, so is the Chief of Police. Get down here quick." The phone went dead.
"Ahhh shit!" Fred stood up quick, "John I gotta go, but you have to come with me. I think Dad's in a bad situation and he's gonna need all the family possible."
"Fred, I've been drinking. I'm in no condition to be of help."
"Then just stay in the car. Emergencies have a way of sobering a guy up really quick." They left Murphy's in the Volvo.

CHAPTER 16

It took twenty minutes to get to the post office. There were already five cars parked near the docks. As he pulled up, Fred saw Mike White standing by Agent James and the Police Chief. Fred stopped the car short of the group and turned to John.

"Whatever you do, stay put until I motion you forward. I don't know how this is gonna go over if they knew you are here. This is supposed to be a kinda crime scene."

"Ok, Ok, but roll the window down a bit, the cold air feels good, it's getting rid of my buzz." Fred got out and walked briskly over to White and the others.

"Hi Mike, what've we got going here?"

White seemed surprised to see Fred. "Ahhh, I don't think you should be involved with this Fred. Roy and Chuck are here and we've plenty of people."

"What do'ya mean? I got a call from you guys and came right over."

"Who called you?"

"Roy did, about twenty minutes ago. What the hell is going on? And why shouldn't I be involved?"

White gave an unhappy look over to where Roy was standing. "Well, he should've checked with me before calling in people."

Fred was getting irritated. "Mike, what the hell is going on!"

"Look Fred, we've got a suspect that has been sneaking around the loading docks tonight checking out the trucks. A security guard approached the person, and the suspect took off running. We're trying to locate whoever it is. The guy was carrying a small handbag. We've had this place under strict lockdown since the bombing and any suspicious activity would be a call for alarm. A couple of the older mail handlers thought they recognized the guy."

"Well Ok Mike, then let's go explore the dock area."

"Hold on Cosman." White put his hand on Fred's chest to stop him.

We have it on good sources that the person might be your dad, that's why I don't want you involved."

Fred froze. He didn't want to believe it, but he knew it was true, it all added up. His dad's behavior, the parts and diagram John found in the basement, it all came together. He couldn't rule it out. You eliminate all the knowns, dates, times, place and names. What's left is the cause, simple deduction.

"Wait a minute Mike, how do you know for sure it's my Dad? You're going on the basis of some old guys. Some old guys that need glasses to read the mailbags. Besides, it's dark out here. How could you or I made a positive ID or even an educated guess?"

"C'mon Fred, don't shit a bullshitter, I've been at this too long. Remember the other day you came into my office? You questioned me about the sentence in one of the reports mentioning 'or relatives active or retired'?"

"Ya, so?"

"Fred, has John complained to you about us asking about him, huh? Well, we've had a tail on him for a while. But as much of a pain in the ass he has been to the post office, all his time is accounted for. That known is eliminated. We had already eliminated the Antifa guys. So, the only known we hadn't eliminated was the retired relative......your Dad. His activities were unaccounted for, and since he was retired, he had no schedule, was hard to pin down. We don't have the resources to watch him twenty-four seven. His whereabouts were unknown. Besides, FBI agent James did some checking. Your dad was an activist on the campus at Ann Arbor Michigan. He was associated with some unfavorable characters, the SDS Weathermen Underground. You know who they are?"

"Ya, I'm aware of them."

"Well tonight, we have a possible ID of a suspect, and I say possible. For the sake of argument, let's say it was someone who may've looked like your Dad. I'll give you that. I had Roy call his house, your mother said he wasn't in, and she didn't know where he went. Therefore, his location is unknown, or is it? Now, I ask you Fred, what would you surmise?"

"Alright Mike, your points are valid, but let me do this. Let me go in there, if, and I say if it is him, I'll call him out. It'll all be over."

"Can't do that Fred. Something happens, my ass is in a wringer, everything comes down on me."

"Mike what the hell do you care? You're already packed up to move on. What the hell do you owe those guys in L'Enfant Plaza? If this comes out good for you, you go out in a blaze of glory. If it doesn't, what do ya have to lose? Screw them, you don't like them or owe them anything."

White looked at Fred and smiled. "Damn, you should have been a motivational speaker or a life coach." Mike hesitated. "Go ahead, you've got fifteen minutes, after that no matter who's in there I'm sending in the troops. Got it?"

"Got it, and thanks Mike."

Fred proceeded cautiously through the parked trucks. Knowing the dock layout helped him navigate near the dock security door in the dark. He had to go up five steps to access the door and onto the open-air dock. Although Postal Inspectors can carry a pistol, Fred had no intention of drawing down if it was his father. He doubted if it was anyone else, they wouldn't be carrying a pistol, Fred just didn't want an incident. He walked slowly in the shadows taking his time, listening for any noise.

A voice in the dark yelled out. "DON'T COME ANY CLOSER!"

"Dad?" There was silence…. Dad!"

"That you Fred?"

"Ya, it's me Dad."

There was a pause. "What're ya doing here son? Get away from here, please."

"What am I doing here? Dad, what are you doing here? Why are you prowling around this dock? Whatever your intention no good can come from this. Too many people have been hurt already. Think of

Mom, she's home worried sick about how you've been behaving."
"I'm sorry about all that……. but this is about family. Besides the post
office killed my Joey. My young Joey. He had his whole life ahead of
him, and they killed him with their god damn safety violations. Well,
they should pay for it. Big time! So, get out'ta here son, no sense both
of us being involved. You don't know what this all about."
"Dad, don't do this! It wasn't the post office, it was Joey."
"What do ya mean it was Joey? WHAT DO YOU MEAN?"
In a softer voice Fred spoke. "Dad…. it was Joey who dismantled the
conveyor belt guard, not the post office."
"YOU'RE LYING! YOU'RE LYING!"
"Noooo Dad. Joey dismantled the safety guard."
"HOW THE HELL DO YOU KNOW THAT? WHERE'S THE PROOF?"
"Dad. Remember Sparks? He worked with Joey on the dock the night
of the accident. He saw Joey taking the guard off. Joey did that a few
nights to get done faster. Sparks was scared to come forward, but he
told John the other night after a union meeting."
"IF THAT'S TRUE, WHY DIDN'T JOHN TELL ME?"
"Dad, he was going to the other night before you guys got into an
argument. He came over to tell you…. but well, you know the rest.
He's out in my car now, Dad please, give it up."
From the darkness Fred heard his dad. "Oh God, what have I done?
I've ruined everything. I could've stopped all of this. I could've told the
officials" There was slight sobbing.
"Dad?"
Fred heard gasping, then in almost a whisper he heard, "Freeee….d!"
John jumped up and ran towards his dad. He found him slumped over
a postal cart used to transport mailbags. He turned his father over.
"DAD! DAD!" His father was breathing hard, barely catching breaths
of air, one hand was on his chest. Fred yelled, "HELP! SOMEONE GET
AN AMBULANCE, HELP!"
The door to the dock burst open, White and the others came running
in, the lights came on.

"Fred, what's going on?"

"It's my dad, I think he's having a heart attack" Fred called out, "SOMEONE CALL AN AMBULANCE, HURRY!" Fred looked down at his dad. "Don't worry Dad, we're getting you some help, hang in there." Wentworth Cosman looked up at his son and gave a faint smile. He lifted his hand to touch Fred's face, it went halfway, he spoke, "I was trying to fix it." There was a sigh, the hand came slowly back down, and the light went from his eyes."

"DAD?" Fred shook his dad. "Dad, fix what?" There was no response. He grabbed his dad up in his arms and sobbed. "Ahh Dad, why, why?" John came pushing through the crowd and knelt down and put his arms around Fred and his dad. For that moment, time stopped and the Cosmans were a family again. White, Roy, and Chuck dispersed the crowd and gave the Cosmans some space and time.

The ambulance came, but to no avail. There was nothing they could do. Few seventy-four-year-old people survive a massive heart attack. The red light of the ambulance grew smaller as it left the parking lot going to University Hospital morgue. Fred stood in silence with John and Mike White. The overhead parking lot light cast their shadows on the pavement.

Mike spoke, "This was a sad thing."

Fred looked up, "Sad and senseless. I think the stress of these past few months took a toll on him."

In turn, Roy, Chuck, Agent James, and the Police Chief walked by and expressed their sentiments. White asked Fred if he could have a quick moment with him. They walked a few paces away.

"Look Fred. I have to make a full report on this. I'll be as respectful and accurate as I can without being harmful."

"I know Mike, ya gotta do what ya gotta do. Thanks for being understanding."

"Fred, take as much time off as you need. Tell John I'll square things with his supervisor." Mike smiled and shook Fred's hand.

Fred and his brother turned and walked towards the Volvo. On the way to the car, John put his arm around his younger brother and pulled him close. "C'mon sport, let's go home."

CHAPTER 17

Fred walked into the reception area and stopped. Allie looked up, came around her desk, and gave him a big, long hug. It had been three weeks since his father passed away on the loading docks. Allie broke away. She held both of his hands and smiled.

"Welcome back Fred. We missed you around here. You look great."

"Thanks Allie, good to see you too."

"Things have been so quiet around here with you gone." Fred started to walk towards his inner office. "I have all your mail organized and recent arbitration folders arranged next to them."

"That won't be necessary Allie. I just came in to pick up my personal belongings."

Allie stared at him. "What do you mean?"

"I'm leaving Allie. I just came up from Mike White's office. There was someone else sitting in his chair. Some guy name Ross Anderson. I introduced myself, handed him my letter of resignation, and left."

"But why? Why are you leaving? Things are back to normal now."

"It's a long story Allie." She sat up on his desk, folded her arms.

"Well, I have all day and I'm getting paid for it, now give."

Fred realized this woman was determined to have her question answered. He went over to the small supply closet and got a cardboard box and came back, bent over, picked up a picture, and placed it inside.

"Well?"

He tried to collect his thoughts, straightened up, and spoke. "That night, three weeks ago, John and I had to go back to the house and tell our mother. When we got there, she was sitting in the kitchen, back straight and legs crossed at the ankles. She had that damn hanky in her hand. It was like she was waiting for us. We approached and she did the darndest thing. She stood up and in a calm low voice said, "I'm going to make some tea." She lit the burner and placed the tea kettle on the fire, came back and sat down. John sat down in one of the kitchen chairs. I just stood there and said, "Mom, I'm sorry."

In her same calm voice, she asked, "Where's your father?" I looked at John, he looked at me.

"Mom, he's gone."

"I know that! When you two came through the door without him, I knew. What I want to know is where did they take him?"

"Allie, I wasn't sure what to say, she caught me off guard with her calm demeanor. I blurted out, University Hospital Morgue."

"Now Fred," she said, "tell me what happened."

"Mom, Dad had a massive heart attack. It caught him quick, and he just died."

"Where were you two?"

"We were right there, Mom, we both held him. He was with us Mom......he was with us."

"Good. Now tell me the rest, everything, I want to know."

"Allie, I almost didn't know who I was talking to. The mother I knew all my life was now the Rock of Gibraltar. I never knew she could be so resilient. Instead of her leaning on John and I for support, we were leaning on her. She was like a wall of support."

In a sweet voice Allie said, "Moms are like that Fred, they save it for when it is needed."

"Well, anyway, I told her everything. She sat there absorbing it like a sponge.... never said anything, she just listened. John wasn't quite sure what to make of it and neither was I. When I was finished, she stood up."

"I think you boys should stay here tonight. You can take your old rooms. We'll talk about arrangements tomorrow. I'm going to make another cup of tea and will be up later. Now you two go."

"Allie, I tell ya, it was like we were ten, and being sent to our rooms. John and I just went upstairs. I laid there for a short period; I could hear her sobbing. I felt so bad for her Allie. The man she spent forty-eight years with, was gone. A lifetime together and all she's left with are memories."

"Fred, in the absence of everything else, for your mom, memories are very comforting."

"I suppose. I don't know anything about that. We buried the ol'man next to Joey, had a small reception afterwards. Mom was glad to see all of Dad's old work buddies there. A lot of people from the post office. Mike White was there, he said headquarters gave him a promotion. Director of the Postal Academy. He actually scoffed when he said that. I asked him what was wrong. That he should be happy. He said he was a victim of the Peter Principle." Fred turned to Allie, "Ever hear of it?" Allie shook her head no. "It was created by a guy named Laurence J. Peter, a Canadian educator. His concept was that a person rises through a corporation until that person hits a level of incompetence. Now some firms may not know what to do with an executive, so they promote the person to a place where they couldn't be effective. Many people who bucked the system, who tried to change the system for the better were moved up and out. An executive who just wanted to improve the system but didn't do it the 'company's way' was moved out. Happens many times. Mike said he got a great 'job' with all the bells and whistles. Only thing is, when you ring the bell or blow the whistle, nothing happens. The weeks after the reception, John and I helped Mom clean out the basement. We fixed things, moved shit around in the garage, basically guy stuff."

"Guy stuff?"

"You know what I mean, we guys get the outside and the basement. You women get everything else."

Allie chimed in, "Oh you mean like the cooking, cleaning, washing, women stuff like that." Fred thought this woman is good at zingers. He'd never want to get in an argument with her.

"We did all that we could to help her. And now I came back to get my stuff."

"But why can't you stay, why do you have to leave? You have so much time invested here."

"No Allie, I'd be ineffective here after what has happened. I'm sort of a pariah here. My career with the postal inspection service is over."

"You didn't do anything Fred. It was your father."

"Doesn't matter Allie, I'm guilty by association, same with John. No, it's better to move on."

"What are your plans, where you gonna go? And what about your brother?"

Fred had been filling the cardboard box as they spoke. It was just about full, he looked around for anything else......nothing.

Allie grabbed his arm and turned him. "Answer my question, what are you gonna do?"

"Oh...mmm I got me an executive security position in California with a tech company, kinda hush, hush government stuff. Mike White, FBI Agent James, and even that stiff collar Chief gave me letters of recommendation. That was better than a gold watch."

"And what about your brother?"

"John? He's going to the University of Minnesota on the GI bill. He'll stay around close to help our mother. He wants to attend law school and be a labor lawyer." Fred smiled, "Won't he be someone's pain in the ass?" Fred leaned on the box and looked at Allie. In all seriousness, John and I are through here. Hell, when I walked through the D dock, I got all kinds of looks."

Allie looked up at him. "I'm going to miss you sailor, you made working here enjoyable. I'm also sorry about the loss of what could've been." She got up on her tiptoes and kissed him on the lips. He returned the embrace thinking this is not so much as a goodbye kiss, but more of 'what could be kiss'. What if he decided to stay? What would that entail? How would their lives be affected? But he decided no, a clean break is better, no loose ends to tie. No lingering afterthoughts. Its best just to leave.

He picked the box up in his arms, said goodbye to Allie, and walked to the elevator. As he stood there, he glanced towards his office. Allie had her back turned, she was crying. Fred felt bad, but he knew that fate is a predator. At times, it doesn't always allow circumstances to occur naturally. It can interfere, causing unrelated elements to combine resulting in an event. People speak about the fickle finger of fate. That's when fate becomes mischievous as if an entity in nature is formed, pushing the boundaries of human understanding and endurance. Fate is not content to ideally watch events unfold, it strikes, taking advantage of elements and causes changes in people's lives. It's fate doing what it does.

In the lobby, he entered into the D dock. He walked slowly, remembering what had happened here some months ago. Passing out through the last door he went into the Minnesota winter. Once again, he was bent forward against the bitter wind, eyes squinted with his hands clasping personal belongings.

CHAPTER 18

The 53-foot Hatteras boat, 'Bamber Breeze', rocked gently on C dock from the waves of a passing boat in the Westpoint Harbor, Redwood City, California. Fred Cosman had a three-day beard growth, was dressed in a blue tank top, khaki shorts, ball cap, and flip flops. He took a sip from his glass of Jameson, tilted his head back to savor the warmth of the liquor going down and to feel the warmth of the sun on his face. The distant seagulls squawked as a charter fishing boat approached the harbor, returning from a day of fishing. The birds knew that a feast of entrails thrown overboard would soon be coming. Following the boat, they'd swoop down low to the vessel circle upwards and repeat the movement. A dozen or so birds were jockeying for the best advantage when the fishermen would clean the fish. Fred enjoyed watching the birds as they did an aerial ballet over the boat. The gentle swaying of the boat and the warmth of the Jameson and sun made Fred a bit loose. His Ray-Ban aviator sunglasses covered his eyes. They were the type of sunglasses that had a silver reflection so no one could see your eyes. The glasses protected him against the sun's glare and the reflection off the water. He also thought that aviator glasses were just plain cool to wear. With his feet up on the railing, Fred was enjoying the three-day July Fourth weekend. Today there were no worries, just the blue California skies and a warm gentle breeze. Fred's only concern was to not fall asleep and get sunburned.

As the charter boat passed by, the captain waved to Fred. Captain Harry Jensen would be over later to have a drink and entertain Fred with stories of fishing with idiot amateurs who thought they were Captain Ahab from the book Moby Dick. They thought surely, they would catch a fish the size of a whale. Most of the time they'd get their lines tangled up, drink too much, and puke overboard. Harry was a retired Navy Master Chief Petty Officer who had 30 years of active duty on almost all naval ships except submarines. He once told Fred, you couldn't catch him on those death tubes for any amount of money. Harry thought it was insane to go under the water when there was plenty of room topside.

He became a civilian a few years back in San Diego, California, drove down to Westpoint, bought a charter boat to begin what he described as the second half of his life. Fred liked Harry, he was down to earth and a straight talker. People down at the Marina office joked that Harry talked so much you would have sworn he was vaccinated with a phonograph needle. When the charter business was slow, Harry would invite Fred out for few days day of fishing. They'd load up one cooler with a few cases of beer and another cooler for bait. Harry took the boat out 10 miles, drop anchor, set the fishing lines, and then he and Fred would sit back and pop a beer. Fred just enjoyed the stories Harry would tell of his time in the Navy, where he had been, men he served with on ship and some of the politics on many ships. Harry told Fred that a corporate board room was not that much different than the bridge of a ship. Officers trying to be the one the captain depended on, tried to catch his favor. Even some of the enlisted men did the same thing to get better assignments. But ninety-nine percent of the men he served with were great guys. Harry would not of traded that life's experience for anything. He was biased, but he felt that America's best men were active or retired servicemen. They were the ones who put everything on the line for God and country, never asking anything in return,

Fred and Harry would stay out for a few days eating the days catch and sleeping on the boat. Harry was divorced; his former wife was a Japanese woman who he met in Osaka, Japan while on leave. She was a pretty woman and Harry married her right away, although he also said that alcohol might have been involved. After several years, she gave up having a husband that was never home. One day she told him to go home to his other woman, the United States Navy. Harry told

Fred that he had to admit she was right, he could never share his life with two people. He packed his bags and went to the one he loved the most. He never remarried but winked that he had a girl in every port. Harry reminded Fred of his father, mainly because they were of the same age. Except for Harry's swagger, he and Wentworth Cosman had a deep inner strength, a presence that attracted people. Fred missed his father immensely.

It had been over a year since Fred had moved to California. He had a position with U.S. Technology, a global software company that had its headquarters based in Silicon Valley. He oversaw 56 security agents. The agents were former FBI, police officers, and high-level military security-type personnel. Fred was impressed with the background of the people he worked with, as a security force they could find a certain piece of straw in a haystack. Their professionalism and diligence were above reproach and he enjoyed working with them.

After his father's death and Fred's separation from the Postal Inspection Service, he sold the condo and all his furnishings. He didn't want to cart furniture across the country, especially since he didn't know where he'd be staying. He packed his personal belongings in his Volvo and drove west.

Fred wanted nothing to remind him of the past. This was a new beginning with a new job, in a new place. He wanted this to be an adventure, one that would help him forget about the troubles of this past year. It was hard leaving his mother knowing that she was alone, but then again, she had his brother John to lean on if she needed assistance. Fred traveled south from St. Paul, on Hwy 35 till he eventually hooked up with Hwy 90 going west. It would be a good ten hours before he reached Rapid City, South Dakota. His plan was to visit Mt. Rushmore, then swing up to historic Deadwood to do some gambling and visit Saloon #10 where Bill Hickok was killed. Then he'd head west on historic Route 66 which would pass through several states. His eventual destination was Las Vegas for a few nights of shows and to make a few deposits in the casinos. His game of choice was blackjack, which in spite of his losses, was entertaining for him. Fred was not going to stay more than a week and then head to Silicon Valley for his new job. This trip was to be his new adventure, a break from his more normal conservative lifestyle. He ended up in Redwood City, California, at the suggestion of a co-worker. Fred was taken aback at the prices of housing. It was not that he couldn't afford buying a house, it just seemed wrong to him spending a large amount just for housing. The guy he was replacing suggested he buy a boat and live on it. Fred could enjoy the boating life as well as waking up to an ocean view each morning. He ended up buying an older 53-foot Hatteras boat which came fully equipped. It didn't take him long to adapt to the marina life. On weekends, he took the boat offshore for a two-day fishing trip. On Sunday afternoon he'd haul anchor and head back to his boat slip at the marina. He'd clean any fish he caught, freeze them, shower, and go to the Marina restaurant for a steak dinner. During the week, he usually worked late, and it was pleasing to know at the end of the day he'd be on his boat relaxing with a drink and letting his concerns be erased by the beautiful sunsets.

While at the Westpoint Marina Restaurant, he met Harry Jensen. Harry was good at entertaining the bar patrons with stories of his naval career and the fishing charter business. He and Harry developed a good friendship. Yet Fred never divulged too much about his past. He felt uncomfortable about anyone knowing how he came to be living in California. Besides, this was to be a new life and Fred didn't want the past to cast a cloud over it. It was enough that he explained that he just wanted a career change. It seemed reasonable to anyone for his move from the Midwest. More and more, Fred became a regular at the Marina Bar. He always sought out Harry and the two would spend the evening with other boaters who made the Marina their home. If Fred wasn't at the Marina Bar, he'd be on his boat or on Harry's. Each took turn taking the other out on fishing trips. Harry always knew the best fishing grounds. The fishing excursions reminded Fred of the many trips to Gull Lake in Brainerd, Minnesota, where his father would take him, John and Joey. Harry became a sort of surrogate father to Fred. It was good to have someone for consul or to look out for him if needed. Fred was totally into his new life.

Work was a nine-to-ten-hour a day for Fred. He usually got to work by six and left between four or five in the evening. The early start allowed him to get a lot of paperwork done before meetings with company executives. He didn't care for the meetings, seeing them as a waste of time and resources. Once a month he would visit one of the company's satellite sites to obtain first-hand accounts of any security problems. He enjoyed these trips where he got to meet many of the people he oversaw. It put him in good standing with those employees as a guy who was not content to sit behind a desk but willing to get out in the field. Fred's boss also appreciated that he brought back current information to the meetings of potential real time security problems. There were always loose ends which Fred would work on from his laptop on the boat. It was a good life and Fred was glad he made the change. Yet he was always concerned about his mother and his brother John. His mother was more homebound now, relying on John more each week. His brother was involved with getting his education, and Fred did feel a bit guilty about John shouldering the total responsibility of their mother's care. Each month, Fred heard less from John, and it bothered him to be out of touch. When he did speak with his brother, he gleamed little from the conversations. The last couple of phone calls, John criticized the post office, saying that it was responsible for the problems of the family. John had made some irrational statements that the bombings was a wakeup call for postal management. Fred was at a loss as to why his brother was obsessed with blaming the post office. Both he and John knew it was their father's action that resulted in the change of their lifestyle. Fred toyed with the concept that perhaps John was unhappy with the way things turned out. That he still had resentment for the way things developed. Fred was beginning to feel that his brother was again showing his hostility towards the postal service, that John's attitude was affecting the man's judgment. It puzzled Fred. He made a mental note about making a trip in the coming months back to St. Paul to visit his mother and have a talk with John.

CHAPTER 19

John was relaxing on his boat, feet up on the boat's railings, having a drink reading a new book when Harry showed up.

"Hey sport, permission to come aboard?"

"Hi ol'timer, ya c'mon aboard, fix yourself a drink. What's up?"

Harry stepped onto the Bambi Breeze, grabbed a beer out of the cooler, and sat down.

"Whatcha reading?"

"A new book called 'An Ugly Angel." It's a story about some young Marine in Vietnam."

Harry took a long sip of beer, then wiped his mouth with the back of his hand. "I tried calling you, but your phone went to voice mail."

"Oh, the damn thing died on me, I'm charging it right now. What's all so important to tear you away from the Marina bar?"

"Your brother John called the asking for you. Said he tried calling you but got no answer. I thought it might be important, so I tried calling you. When it went to voice mail, I thought it strange. I told him I'd go down to your boat and get ya."

Fred put the drink and book down and sat upright. "Did he say what he wanted? Was he anxious?"

"Well, the bartender answered the phone, when he didn't see you, he yelled over to me asking if I knew where you were. I shook my head no, then he asked me to take the call. I told your brother who I was and made the phone call. When ya didn't answer, I came right down."

Fred thanked Harry, then both went back to the Marina Bar so Fred could make a call.

The phone rang three times before John answered.

"Hello?"

"John, it's me Fred, what's going on?"

"Hi Fred, sorry, I didn't recognize the phone number, there was no name on the screen."

"I'm calling from the Marina Bar, my cell phone was dead, it was being charged. What's going on? It's kinda unusual for you to call during the week."

"Well, it's Mom, she had a small stroke a few hours ago and I had to take her to the University Hospital."

"John, how's she doing? How bad is it?"

"Ah, the doctors said she's stable now. They gave her some blood thinner stuff, anticoagulant, I think. She is resting and seems better. I'm at the hospital now, she's sleeping now so I might head home."

"Has this happened before John? I mean, has she been having difficulties?"

"She's had a few dizzy spells. I took her to see the doctor the other day. They said it was low blood pressure. The doctors explained that blood pressure can rise or fall during the day depending on what you did, maybe exercising, maybe standing too long, it can even happen after a meal. They said many older people get postprandial hypotension. So, it might have been an age thing. Doctors didn't want to give her any drugs right now, they thought it was best to monitor her, recommended her not to exert herself, that kind of thing."

"Maybe I should get on a flight out there or should I wait a bit, what do ya think John?"

"Well, we wouldn't want you to miss the California's warm weather and sun, now, would we?"

"What the hell are you talking about John? What's with the attitude? I am asking for your advice, is Mom's condition serious enough for me to come out right now, or should I wait a bit and come out for a longer visit?"

"Is her condition serious enough? Christ Fred, she's in the hospital! How serious do you want it to be? You want to wait and come back for a funeral? It's your decision sport, you decide."

"That was uncalled for big brother, you know what I meant. What the hell is wrong with you?" There was a pause. Fred could hear a sigh. In a depressed voice, he heard his brother.

"I don't know Fred. It's just seeing Mom laying there in the hospital bed; I got really worried. Everything's changed, Dad's gone, dead from a heart attack, and now Mom suffers a stroke, you're out there in California…. I'm battling my head at school, working part time, caring for Mom. It gets to be a bit much at times. No more Sunday dinners sport."

Fred could sense the despondence in his brother's voice. Perhaps things were coming down on John, the sense of loss from what the family had, and a longing for the way things used to be. Could this be why John has been criticizing the post service? Everything the family had experienced, in some way involved the post office. The postal jobs they all had, Joey's death, and their father's death, all connected to the post office. And finally, both brothers leaving the post office due in part to the postal bombings. The family's tragedy was all linked to the post office. A series of individual events caused a tight knit family to become dysfunctional. Fate had intervened. After the phone call with his brother, Fred confided in Harry, and both agreed that Fred should immediately take a trip back to Minnesota. John needed assistance in coping with the family's situation.

Fred booked a 9 a.m. Delta flight leaving out of San Francisco. He'd be in Minneapolis within three and a half hours. He was going to ask John to pick him up but, decided a rental car would give him more freedom and limit depending on his brother for transportation. He had Harry look after his boat. Landing at the airport, he caught bus transportation over to the Hertz rental counter. He also chose not to stay at his parent's house. He felt he needed the option of space from his mother and brother, so he booked a room at the Hilton near the Mall of America in Minneapolis, just off Highway 494. After getting situated in his room, he drove over to the University Hospital to visit his mother. The woman at the front desk directed him to where his mother was. Upon entering the room, Fred was taken aback at how frail she looked. Gone were the rosy cheeks and full face. What he saw was an old woman who in one year seemed to have aged greatly.

There was still beauty in the face, but the thin cheeks and whiteness contrasted with the way he remembered her. He walked quietly over to her bedside, leaned over, and kissed her on the forehead. She made a slight murmur as she slept. Fred stepped back. He saw the chair next to the bed and sat down. He wondered what the hell they were going to do. It had been three days since her stroke, and it appears she wasn't responding well to the bed rest and medication. As he sat there, a doctor walked in.

"Hello there, I'm Dr. Benson the attending physician for Mrs. Cosman."

"How's she doing Doc? She looks really frail."

"Yes, well older people sometimes have difficulty recovering from a stroke. When your Mrs. Cosman came to us, she was slightly dehydrated and underweight. I suspect she hasn't been eating much, nor drinking much liquid. We've been able to get liquid into her intravenously, and she has eaten a bit when she's awake. There appears to be no long-term effect from the stroke, but time will tell."

"But why hasn't she responded? I can understand if she was by herself, but she is getting care now."

"I'm sorry, I didn't ask who you were. Are you family?"

"Yes, I'm her son."

"I didn't know she had another son. I met John, but he didn't mention you."

"Well, I have been out in California and just heard about her stroke and caught the first available flight out."

"Ok, I just wanted to make sure I wasn't giving out information to non-family members. We expect her to be coming around with treatment, like I said, for some it takes time."

"When do you think she'll be able to go home?"

"Um, perhaps a few days. I just want a few days for her to better respond to the treatment. And I do expect her to respond better."

"OK, thanks Doc. Will she be waking up soon? I'd like her to know I'm here."

"Well, she is sleeping well and that's a great medicine only nature can provide. I think she'll be awake around 4 p.m. We usually wake her for mealtime and to check her vitals." Fred looked back at his mother, then turned to the doctor.

"Guess I'll go do some errands, check in with my brother and make some phone calls. Thanks again Doc." Fred went over, kissed his mother on the forehead again, and left.

He wasn't sure what to do first, but he sure in hell wanted to talk to his brother. It bothered him a great deal that John hadn't mentioned him to the doctors. He could excuse John being overwhelmed by their mother's stroke, but at some point, John could have mentioned there was another son. He also wondered if John had told his mother he was coming from California. Was John unconsciously excluding him to others as a family member? The last phone call with his brother made Fred think John was a bit resentful. Fred was free to start a new life in California while John had the responsibility of caring for their mother while attempting to carve out a new life for himself. Added to the possible resentment was that John would run into people who were aware of the family's troubled past. He could no longer go to the VFW post or Murphy's Bar without people looking at him. Friendships were dissolved to eliminate the awkward feeling that people would judge him because of his father. Fred realized he had no such problems. Everyone he met had no idea of his past. He knew he could come and go without being judged. Fred started to see things in a new light. He saw that John was burdened with obstacles he himself didn't experience. He decided to test the water and see how people felt about the family.

It was close to 2 o'clock and Fred headed to the VFW post for a drink and to kill some time before he visited his mother. He pulled his rental car into the VFW parking lot, got out and took a deep breath before going in. The place hadn't changed, and he thought why should it. It had been slightly over a year since he was last in the joint. There were two guys he didn't recognize at the bar. He walked down to the end.

A familiar face came walking towards him with a smile.

"Why Fred Cosman, how the hell ya doing guy?"

Fred smiled back. "Good Max, and yourself?"

"Better than I have a right to. Where ya been keeping yourself? What's it been a year, year and a half?"

"Ya, it's been close to a year and a half. I'm living out in California now. Great weather and you should see the women Max. The ladies would love ya."

"Ah, not for this old dog Fred. The last time I looked at a shapely woman, my ol' lady took her teeth out and threw them at me." Both men chuckled. "What'll you have?"

"How about a few fingers of Jameson?"

Max smacked the edge of the bar with his fingers. "Jameson it is." He threw a small bar towel over his shoulder and walked off.

Fred was looking around the bar when he felt a tap on his shoulder. He turned around and heard……

"Buy me a drink sailor?"

" Allie!" He got up and gave her a big hug lifting her off the floor.

"Wow, you're the last person I thought I'd see here. What're you doing off work so early? And in a bar no less."

"I took a few days off to extend the weekend. Saving my vacation time for the summer. I'm just here with the girls for an early drink; then we're going to dinner." Fred looked Allie over.

"Damn Allie, you look great, new hair style and all."

Allie patted the side of her hair. "Glad you noticed. A woman needs a change every so often. But what about you? What are you doing here and where have you been?"

Max came back with his drink. "This one's on the house Fred, good to see ya back."

"Thanks Max, good to see you too." Fred took a sip of his drink and spoke. "Well, first of all I'm living on a boat in California and have a pretty good job. Had a call from my brother a few days back. Our mother had a slight stroke, and I thought my place should be here. At least for a while, so I took some time off."

"Oh, sorry to hear about your mother Fred. It must have been hard for her this past year and all."

"Ya, she's a bit frail, and it looks like she hasn't held up well, especially after…. well, you know."

"Oh, don't worry Fred, nobody even talks about that. It's old news anyway. So, were you even gonna call and say hi? Hell, I haven't even gotten so much as a postcard. You…, just up and disappeared."

"I just got back today, unpacked my bags, went to see my mother, and came here for a drink. I'm gonna go see her after this drink."

"Well look, here's my phone number, call me and we can have a drink and catch up."

"Won't your girlfriends talk?"

Allie smiled. "Let them, I don't work for you anymore." She turned and walked back to her table. Her girlfriends were huddled looking over at Fred. He knew they were asking Allie about him. She said something to them, then turned and smiled at him. Fred raised his glass to them and finished the last of the Jameson.

It took Fred almost an hour to get through the Minneapolis rush hour traffic to the hospital. When he pulled into the parking lot, he spotted John's blue pickup truck. He thought to himself, oh boy, this is going to be interesting. He got off the elevator on the fourth floor and made his way to his mother's room. As he walked in, his mother's eyes widened.

"Fred! When did you get here?" She held out her arms to greet him.

"Hi Mom." He went over and gave his mother a long hug, the first one in over a year.

"I came in this afternoon, you were sleeping. I met your doctor and he said you'd be awake about this time."

"Why didn't you let me know you were coming?" Fred looked over at John, who didn't look happy to see him. "Well things happened so fast, I heard about your stroke and came on the first available flight. Had to tighten up a few things first, but here I am."

"Oh, you shouldn't have bothered yourself, I'm ok. The doctor is taking real good care of me, and the nurses are really sweet. There's probably a few that might be interested in you and John." Fred looked down at his frail mother and thought, with her having to deal with her medical problems, all she can think about are her sons. He looked over to his brother.

"Hello John." His brother just looked at him and said hi. Fred thought he could deal with this later and turned his attention back to his mother.

"How ya feeling Mom? The doctor said you could probably leave in a few days."

"I'm feeling much better than I did a few days ago. It was probably just another dizzy spell that brought this on. All this fuss because of that."

"Mom, you do realize you had a stroke, right?"

"Oh, they can call it what they want, I'll be fine."

Fred smiled at the resilience of his mother, she was frail, but she still had some fire in her.

"Did you put your stuff in the house? Your old room is all made up. Of course, you may have to dust a few things." His mother smiled weakly. Fred could still see the beauty in the women's face.

"Naw Mom, I didn't want to be a bother, so I got a room nearby not far from the hospital. I'll be ok."

"Well, it doesn't seem right for you to spend good money when there's your old room not being used. In fact, why don't you and John stay with me for a while? I can cook you both a good Sunday dinner like we used to have. It'll be good to have the two of you around again." Fred smiled at his mother and patted her hand.

"We'll talk about it later Mom, in a few days." He looked up at John who hadn't said a thing. Just then the doctor walked in with two nurses.

"Hello Mrs. Cosman, how are we feeling today?" He then turned to the Cosman brothers and spoke. "Well gentlemen, if you excuse us, I have to examine your mother and take some blood work. You can come back at eight for extended visiting hours."

Both brothers said goodbye to their mother and left. Outside the room Fred turned to his brother. "John, did I do something to piss you off? During this whole visit you didn't say a thing. I felt like you were angry that I showed up. And another thing, why didn't you tell Mom I was coming or even the doctor, hell he didn't even know there was another son. What the hell is going on?" Fred stood there for what seemed like a long awkward moment before his brother spoke.

"I'm sorry sport, did I hurt your feelings? Did I fail to jump up and down when you arrived? The distant son makes a royal showing. He arrives after over a year's absence and wants to be greeted by all."

"Wait a minute, John!"

"No! You wait. You come waltzing in here from out west. You're living the good life out there. New job, new beginning, ya come back here and what? You expected to be greeted with open arms? You didn't have the courtesy during this year and a half to call me and ask if there's some way you could help. Maybe come back and visit with Mom? Let me get some time to myself. Hell, I don't mind being here for Mom, but it would have been grand if you at least offered the help. You're out there in California, you didn't have to deal with what I've been through. Hell, after Dad died, I felt like I had leprosy. I couldn't go to Murphy's or the VFW without people feeling awkward talking to me. The guys from the union distanced themselves from me. The very guys I helped many times. I'd be out in Mom's yard doing some work and the neighbors would go inside. I was Mom's only contact. I could deal with all the jerks who shunned me. What hurt was to see how Mom's spirit was going down. I wondered what she thought about her husband. All because of what I did.........I, I mean of what had happened and what it did to this family."

Fred stepped back, "What did you do?"

John ran his hand through his hair and looked at the floor. "Nothing, I just spoke out of line. It's been hell this past few days, I just got confused."

Look John, I'm sorry about what you had to go through after Dad died, but I didn't cause it. I know I could've offered some assistance, but you never let on there was any difficulty. Ever since we were kids, you took charge, you never let me really take the lead, always the big brother. I had no idea things weren't kosher."

John looked Fred straight in the face. "You could've asked." John turned and walked away.

CHAPTER 20

It was six thirty when Fred arrived back at the Hilton. He was headed to the elevator when he decided to go to the bar for a drink. Walking in, he took the middle chair. A young bartender came over and put a coaster and napkin on the bar.

"What will it be sir?"

"Give me two fingers of Jameson." Fred took a handful of the snack mix from a bowl and popped it in his mouth. He looked up to watch the WCCO news on the television. The bartender came back and placed the Jameson on the coaster.

"Thanks."

"Yes sir, did you want to order any food? The kitchen closes in an hour."

"No, I don't think so." He looked back up at the television when a news alert came on. As the commentator was announcing a recent bombing at the post office, the screen shifted to the very post office Fred had worked at. He hesitated as he raised the glass of Jameson. In an almost hectic voice, Fred called over to the bartender.

"Hey guy, can you turn that up?" Fred was almost mesmerized as he listened to the announcer at the scene describe how less than an hour ago a bomb went off at the St. Paul Post Office. A visual of the bomb site was shown. Police were seen masking off the area with yellow police tape. A large group of people were milling around firetrucks and ambulances. The announcer was heard explaining that a little past five o'clock, a bomb exploded at the D dock. No explanation for the bombing was known as investigators were examining the area. In his mind, Fred was brought back to that day almost two years ago when he was investigating the first bombing. The image of finding Anthon's body under the mail bags flashed in his mind. It was almost like it happened yesterday. As he looked closer, he recognized a familiar face, Roy Downing, his former colleague at the Postal Inspection

Service. Roy was being interviewed by the television announcer.
"We have here Postal Inspector Roy Downing, the head Inspector for
the St. Paul Post Office. Tell me, Inspector Downing, do you have
anything you can tell us about the bombing?" Roy looked briefly down
at his notes.

"We've been able to piece together that the bombing only did
structural damage, no one was hurt in the blast. At the time of the
explosion, the dock crew was on a lunch break, so we're grateful for
that. We haven't had time to find evidence of the bomb since it just
happened an hour ago, but we will find something, we always do.
Now if you'll excuse me, I have to get back to the investigation."

"Yes, thank you Inspector Downing. Well, as you can see viewers, it's
still too early for a complete understanding of the events here at the
St. Paul Post Office. There will be a full report on the nine o'clock
news." Fred stared at the television screen. He then noticed another
familiar face, St. Paul Police Chief Pat Harrison talking to Roy Downing.
Fred sat back in his chair and thought, so the old gang is back together.
The television went back to the regular WCCO news, Fred finished his
drink and left the bar. He went up to his room and threw his coat on
the bed, walked into the bathroom, turned the water on, and splashed
it on his face. Walking over to the window, he looked out over
Minneapolis. It was starting to get dark, and the lights of the city were
coming on. Fred remembered how he always liked the view of a city at
night, it had a certain charm to him. He felt antsy and wasn't sure
what to do. It was only eight o'clock, so he went over the phone and
dialed a number. A female voice came on the line.

"Hello?"

"Allie? It's Fred."

"Well, hi, I didn't expect you to call this soon, what's up?"

"I just got back to the hotel, had a drink in the bar. Went to visit my
mother earlier, John was there."

"How's she doing? Any good news to report?"

"She seems to be stable. She was awake when I arrived. It was good

to see her. Now John was another matter." Fred rubbed his forehead.
"Why? What's the matter? You must have been happy to see him."
"Ahh, I was, sort of. He seemed upset with me, hardly spoke while we
were in my mother's room. Outside her room, he gave me an earful.
Look, I know it's short notice, but I'm not tired and don't know what to
do with myself, do you think you'd be up for a drink?"
"Well with that kind of invitation how could a girl resist?"
"I know, it's not the best I could do. If you think it's not a good idea, I'll
understand."
"No, no, you're not backing out that easy. Besides, it sounds like you
need someone to talk to, and I am on vacation."
"Ok, where do you want to meet?"
"Fred, there's no sense in both of us driving around town and you did
mention your hotel had a bar. Why don't we meet there?"
"I'll see you in a little bit."
Allie found Fred in a booth at the back of the Hilton Bar. He already
had an empty glass in front of him. She slid in beside him and looked
at the glass.
"So, it's going to be one of those nights?" Fred smiled and looked
down at his glass.
"No, I just didn't feel right just sitting here taking up space, and the
bartender has to make a living." Fred motioned the bartender over.
"What'll you have folks?" Allie ordered a glass of Malbec wine, and he
ordered another Jameson. The bartender came back shortly and
placed the drinks on the table and a small bowl of snack mix.
"You know, your new hair style really looks good on you. I've never
seen you with short hair."
"Thanks Fred, that's two compliments in one day from you, but you
didn't call me to talk about my hair." Fred turned his drink glass a few
times with his fingers.
"I don't know Allie, coming back here, things are so familiar, yet I don't
know what to do. When I lived here, I could always find something to
occupy myself with, but now......."

"Hell, Fred you just arrived today, you're here to see your mother, what do you expect? It's not like anything is expected of you. Cheers."
They both raised their glasses and took a sip.
"By the way Allie, did you see the news tonight?"
"No, I was at dinner with my girlfriends. I was going to watch the nine o'clock news."
"There was a bombing at the St. Paul Post Office, the D dock no less."
"What! A bombing? When? Was anybody hurt?"
"No, the mail handlers were on a lunch break when it happened. I caught the news on that television." Fred pointed to the bar. "I saw Roy Downing and Chief Police Harrison. They were investigating the bombing."
"Wow, you talk about de' ja' vu. What did they say about the bombing?"
"Not much they could tell, only that nobody was hurt, that it was mostly structural damage. Roy got interviewed, and since it just happened, there wasn't much to report."
"You know Roy is my new boss? He took over shortly after you left. He's good to work for, doesn't have your knack for getting to the, what did you call it, eliminating the knowns and what's left is the cause."
"Damn, you remember that huh?"
"You betcha, and much more." Fred looked puzzled but didn't say anything. "Besides the bombings, what else has you rattled?"
"It's this thing with my brother. He laid it on me that…. that I kinda skipped town after my father died. Left him caring for our mother, which he really doesn't mind. He implied that I took the easy way and left, started a new life while he was here dealing with the family's disgrace."
"Oh, hell Fred, what could you do? You said your career with the Inspection Service was basically over, you got a good job offer and took it. Who could blame you for that?"
"Well, John does. Plus coming back here, my mother having a stroke, and now this bombing. It's brings back memories of a difficult time.

And there is something John's not telling me, not sure what. I admit I was having it good out there in California, good job, living on a boat at the marina, meet some good people."

"Meet any women?"

Fred smiled. "No, no women. Heck, most of the women at the marina are married or too young, I mean co-ed young. Besides, work has me going on trips or I work late. I spend most of my time on the boat. Sometimes I do work from the boat, once in a while go out fishing. I met this great guy; he runs a fishing charter service. He's a retired Navy guy, quite a character, he regales the patrons at the Marina Bar with all kinds of stories. He reminds me of my father, you'd love him."

"I wouldn't mind meeting him." Allie had a curious smile and took another sip of her drink. The pair continued to have a few drinks while talking about past work, living in California versus Minnesota. Allie expressed her attitude that she could live anywhere as long as she had a good job. Fred said she might enjoy the west coast lifestyle. It was laid back, great weather, and of course there was always the ocean. The bar was empty except for Fred and Allie. The happy hour crowd left a long time ago and only the two remained. Allie mentioned to Fred that they had been sitting there for two hours.

"I'm sorry Allie, I didn't realize it was getting late. Didn't mean to keep you this long. It's just been nice to see ya and talk."

"No problem, after all I am on vacation, sort of. It's just that........." She hesitated.

"What? Have I been going on too long? Have a lot on my mind and I just needed to vent a bit."

"Well, it's just that when you called, I was glad. Thought you just wanted to get together and make up for lost time."

"I did, it's just good to see you." Allie looked at him.

"Fred. Look, you think I came over just to pass time catching up?"

"Whaat?"

"Don't make this awkward for me. I came over because I wanted to be with you. Do I have to spell it out?" She tilted her head slightly and raised her eyebrows.

He looked at her and realized he had been an idiot. Smiling he said, "Well I do have a mini-bar in my room." Allie's body language was that of relief as she grabbed her purse and slid to get out of the booth. "Ya know Fred, sometimes you can be a bit slow."

They left the hotel bar and walked to the elevator. He pushed the button for the fourth floor. In the room, he made them drinks, Vodka tonic for her and a small Jameson for himself. The lights of the city was their view out the window. It was sort of picturesque, the dim city lights set the mood. He reached over, took her drink, and kissed her. The scent of her perfume was more intoxicating than the drinks. Fred could not remember lips that soft. The drinks had already dampened any inhibitions they may have had, and their embrace seemed long overdue as the passion increased. They moved over to the bed while slowly undressing each other. The love making was long, slow, and deliberate. She was passionate, and his excitement was met by hers. Afterwards, they laid in each other's arms.

Turning slightly to him, she said, "I thought it could be like that."

"Well, over the years I wondered about that, that is, what it might be like. But we had boundaries. Besides, it wouldn't have been fair to you, us working together and all. Things like that don't seem to work out."

"I know, there were times I thought the same thing." Fred looked at her sort of quizzical. She looked back at him, "What? You don't think women think of these things also?"

"Nooo, it's just that......"

"Just what......?"

"Well, I guess it catches a guy off guard to think women feel like that." She playfully smiled and adjusted the sheets, "We can, and do, so there." Fred was grinning as he stroked her hair. "Hmpf, you guys think you're so smart." They both fell asleep with a slight grin on their face.

The sun's glare woke Fred. He stretched and yawned. He noticed that Allie was not in bed. He heard water running in the bathroom. Allie came walking out adjusting the buttons on her top.

"Morning sleepyhead. You gonna lay there all morning?" Fred blinked his eyes, yawned again, and stretched his head.

"What time is it?" Fred started to reach over to end table.

"It's eight thirty. You were snoring for the last half hour."

He smiled, "I was calling out your name." She threw a pillow at his head. He was still smiling.

"Where're you going? I thought you were on vacation."

"I am, but a girl can't be seen leaving a hotel too late, doesn't look good. You have time for coffee?"

"I'd like to, but I should shower and shave and get over to the hospital. It'll be about nine-thirty or ten before I get there. I'll get some coffee to go in the restaurant downstairs. How about you?" Allie finished buttoning her top and tucked it in her pants.

"I'll probably do the same thing. I have a bunch of errands to run and some groceries to pick up." She walked over to the mirror and brushed her hair. "So, what are your plans after seeing your mother? You going to visit with your brother John?"

Fred was sitting on the edge of the bed now rubbing his forehead, his head was bent, he looked up. "Don't know. John didn't seem very happy with me. I might have to have a sit-down with him and hash things out." Allie picked up her purse and kissed him.

"Well, if you get bored, give me a call. We can have dinner tonight, providing you're good with that." Fred got up, put his trousers on, and walked Allie to the door.

CHAPTER 21

The Minneapolis traffic was light, and Fred got to the hospital within thirty minutes. He got in the elevator and went to the fourth floor. The doctor was in his mother's room as Fred entered. His mother was being administered to by a nurse. She had a blood pressure cuff around her arm.

"Morning Doc, how's my mother doing?"

"Morning Mr. Cosman, oh she's doing fine, responding well to everything we give her. I believe the rest has really helped her." His mother smiled at Fred.

"Morning Mom. He went over and gave her a kiss on the forehead. "Sounds like you'll be up on your feet pretty soon." She adjusted her sheets after the nurse took the blood pressure cuff off.

"Oh, I don't know about that, but I do feel so much better, and I'm ready to go home." Fred noticed her voice sounded stronger and her complexion was better.

"What'da ya think Doc, will our girl be ready to go home?" The doctor finished writing on her medical chart, clicked the pen, and put in into his pocket.

"Well, if her tests come back looking good today, which I believe they will, tomorrow might not be out of line." The doctor turned and walked out.

"See that Mom, the doctor said you're good to go." He smiled affectionately at her.

"Let's see what tomorrow brings Fred, I don't want to get my hopes up."

"Say mom, was John in?"

"He came in earlier. He has an afternoon class and needs to get his books and stuff from his place. Said he'd come back tonight." She hesitated a bit before she spoke. "Fred be straight with me, is there conflict between you and John? You two seemed tense the other day when you were both here."

Fred didn't want his mother to concern herself and possibly have her blood pressure go up, so he lied. "No Mom, it's just my older brother, being an older brother, he likes to take charge and all that. We're good."

"Well, I'm glad. I don't think my boys should fight or have disagreements. Especially since you haven't seen each other for a year."

Fred felt sheepish about lying to his mother, but he felt it wouldn't help her situation to tell her the truth. The nurse came back with medication for his mother.

"Sorry Mr. Cosman, but your mother needs to take her medications and get some sleep. The nurse put a tray down and handed his mother some pills. "She'll probably get sleepy now. But there are afternoon visiting hours."

"OK. Mom, I'm gonna head out and do some errands, I'll catch up with you later this afternoon." He kissed her forehead. She did appear to be a bit drowsy.

"Alright son. I do feel a bit tired." His mother closed her eyes.

Fred walked out, went down in the elevator into the lobby, and stood there. He thought, so what the hell do I do until later? What do you do in a city you're visiting to kill time? It was then that he decided to call his former protégé Inspector Roy Downing. Fred was curious about the postal bombing from the other night. He felt that perhaps Roy might indulge him in thoughts on it. He drove back to the Hilton, went up to his room, and first ordered room service, then he called Roy. The phone rang three times before Roy answered.

"Hello, Inspector Roy here."

"Roy, hi, Fred Cosman here." There was a pause on the line.

"Fred?" There was a shorter pause. "Fred, how the hell are you? This is a pleasant surprise. Where are you?"

"Actually, I'm in Minneapolis right now. I am visiting my mother."

'Wow, you talk about a voice from the past. How long you gonna stay? Any chance of meeting up?" Fred was caught off guard by the quick invitation. He half expected Roy to be a bit leery, but Roy's response made him feel more relaxed.

"Whoa, slow down Roy, didn't expect the rapid-fire questions but sure, why not, let's meet at the Hansen VFW post 295."

"Ya, that'll be good. Say tonight about six thirty? Traffic will be lighter, and I can get there quicker."

"Fine, I'll be looking forward to seeing you, Roy." Fred hung up the room phone and looked out the hotel window. He stared at the Minneapolis landscape. He wondered if he was doing the right thing, reopening contact with a former colleague. Also, he felt a bit guilty for his motive of getting information on the recent bombing. But he had to know the particulars. Was it a copycat action or newer activity by some group? The bombing site, and the similarities bothered him. There was also the ethics of Roy possibly divulging any sensitive information. Roy would have every right in telling Fred to buzz off. He could almost hear the manner that Fred himself would use if anyone tried that with him. After the phone call with Roy, Fred finished off the sandwich he had ordered from room service, grabbed his coat, and headed out the door. He needed to talk with his brother, straighten things out, but certainly not at the hospital. It was well past two o'clock, so Fred went to the University Hospital to visit his mother. He found her sitting up talking to the doctor.

"Hi Mom, hi doc. Any good news?" The doctor turned his head and smiled at Fred.

"Things look real great Fred. All her vitals are stable, and her lab work is good. I believe your mother can be discharged today if she is up for it." The doctor turned back to Mrs. Cosman, looked down at her, and smiled. "You've been a real good patient. We're going to miss you around here." He patted her hand and walked out. Fred walked closer to his mother.

"Well Mom, you're breaking out of here, are you up for it? I bet you'll be glad to get back home." She looked up at him and said, "Yes, I'm

ready to sleep in my own bed and maybe do a little house cleaning."
"Oh no Mom, you should take it easy for a few days to get used to a
routine. After all, you've been laid up in bed for these few days and
you don't want to push things."
"Nonsense Fred, a little activity is just what I need to loosen up these
old bones. Besides, I want to have a Sunday dinner with you and your
brother just like we used to."
"Now that you mentioned him, has John been in?"
"No, he called a little while back, said he has some things to do and will
be in around five or so. He's so busy with school and work. He's doing
really good, but......" She paused and looked down at her hands.
"But what Mom?"
"John seemed a bit distracted these past few weeks. I figured it was
schooling, work, and helping me. Yet at times I see him staring off like
he's trying to remember something, and he has been rummaging
around in the basement. Sometimes he stays down there for a while
like your father did, fooling around with stuff. I asked him what he was
doing down there, he just said he was straightening things out.
Anyway, at times he doesn't seem himself, but then again it could be
my imagination." Fred took this all in.
"Look Mom, John doesn't know about you being discharged today, I'll
give him a call." Fred dialed his brother's cell phone, but it went to
voice message. "Say John, Mom's doctor is letting her out today. I'm
here and will get her home. Call me right away when you get this
message." Fred hung up and put his cell phone in his pocket.
"Well, Mom, seems John's unable to answer. I'll have the nurse get
your belongings, and she can help you dress, and we'll get you home."
The nurse was notified and came with Mrs. Cosman's belongings. Fred
and his mother left the hospital and he drove her home. It was five
o'clock by the time they arrived at her house, and Fred got his mother
settled in. He was concerned that John had not returned his call. His
mother got up to make some tea. She put the tea kettle on the stove.
"Fred, will you get the smoked shoulder out of the freezer in the

cellar? Oh, and get a few cans of peas." She smiled. "I'm going to make a nice Sunday dinner for you two."

Fred opened the cellar door, turned the light on and went downstairs. He looked around and was surprised at how clean things looked. He thought, wow, John really has been cleaning up down here. The years of stuff his father had collected were gone except for two cardboard boxes, and a few tools on the worktable. He figured the boxes contained junk for the garbage man on Friday. He got the smoked shoulder and peas and started to head back up when he noticed a familiar scent. He tilted his head and thought that perhaps it was the smell from cleaning stuff John had used. After he put the groceries on the kitchen counter, his mother spoke up.

"Fred, is there something bothering you? Ever since we got back home, you've been looking at your watch." He turned to his mother. "Not really, Mom. I was supposed to meet a friend at the VFW at six-thirty, but it's not a big deal."

"Oh, go meet your friend, I'll be fine. I'm sure your brother will be coming over soon." No sooner had Fred said, "I'll wait till he comes," then John walked through the door. His mother turned and smiled at him.

"Hi Mom, how does it feel to be back home?" He walked up to her and gave her a kiss. Fred looked at him with a pissed off look. When their mother went into the living room, Fred approached him.

"Where the hell have you been? I called you two hours ago." John walked away from Fred.

"Get off my back sport, I had things I had to do. Besides, Mom wasn't supposed to come home today. I was going to visit her at the hospital."

Fred trailed after him, "But I left you a phone message, and why did it go to voicemail?"

"The damn thing was dead, I had to recharge it. Now back off!"

"What? That was the only phone in town?" John turned and stood his ground.

"Look sport, I said I had things to do, and that I had planned to visit her in the hospital."
Fred took a breath and tried to regain his composure. "Look, I have to meet a friend. Can you stay with Mom 'til I get back?"
In a patronizing voice John said, "Sure sport, I'll cover you again."
Instead of replying, Fred left the house.

It was a little past six o'clock when Fred entered the VFW. He was surprised to see that Roy was already there. As he walked over, Roy gave him a big smile. He got up and shook Fred's hand and clapped him on the left shoulder with his other hand.
"How ya doing Fred? Christ you look great. That California weather is doing you good."
Fred responded, "The best part is that you don't have to shovel it." He sat down in a chair next to Roy.
"Well, you're right with that pal. Wow, I can't believe how good you look, sun tanned and everything." A waitress came over and took their order.
"Ya the weather is great out there, sun, sun, and more sun. Plus, I live on a boat at a marina. It's pretty damn nice."
Roy got a little serious. "Geez Fred, sorry to hear about your mother. How's she doing?"
"She's doing fairly good. I took her home from the hospital and she's settled in. My brother John is staying with her right now."
"Good to hear that, Fred. So, what are your plans while you're back here?" The waitress came back with their drinks, and they both took a sip.
"I really have no plans. Just came back because of my mother. Not sure how long I'll stay, maybe a week or two, but eventually I have to get back to my job."
"Good. Maybe we can get together again for a few drinks? Quite frankly I was surprised when I got your call. I mean, out of the blue a voice from the past calls." Roy smiled and slapped Fred on the back. "It's really good to see ya."

Fred shifted uncomfortably in his chair. He was looking down at his two hands clasping his glass. "Ya, well about that Roy. It was no accident I called. I was watching the news on the hotel TV and saw the news about the latest bombing at the post office. You can understand how it caught my attention. I ran into Allie at the VFW. She said she worked for you now. That you were now in charge of cases like we did a few years back." Roy looked at him with a bit of surprise.

"You ran into Allie? Mmm, I thought she took off for some place on vacation. But ya, I have your old job. I report to a guy named Ross Anderson. He took White's old job. Not, a bad guy to work for. He assigns you some projects and then stays off your back. Hey, remember that case you had? Some guy named Zimmerman, a financial manager." Fred searched his memory.

"Oh, ya I remember him. Didn't the post office try to stick him with paying for the funds of a contract station that went bankrupt?" Roy gave a little smile. "Well, the post office lost out on that one. Zimmerman's case went to arbitration, and he won. The PO had to pay him back his whole retirement plus damages. The managers who pressed that case against him got reamed. I think one of them got demoted or put out to a low-level Postmaster position. Boy, you talk about justice being served."

Fred knew that case well and was glad this Zimmerman guy made out well. However, he didn't want to rehash old cases with Roy, and decided to cut to the chase.

"Look Roy, I'm wondering if you're able to share any information about this latest bombing. It seems like the ones we were involved in. Was it a copycat bombing or anything related to that old case?" Roy scratched his head, looked down at his drink and then he looked at Fred.

"Look guy, I really shouldn't be commenting on an ongoing case. However, since it just happened and it hasn't really been assigned to me, I can tell you what I suspect. Yes, it is almost like the bombing case we worked on. As far as I know, we haven't gotten back any forensic report from the FBI. Anyway, the place and type of explosion seems to duplicate what we went up against." Roy took a sip of his drink.

Fred spoke up, "Are there any suspects or groups that are being looked at?"

Roy looked at Fred, "Just the usual suspects, groups, Antifa, any local radical groups. But look Fred, if you think this might be connected to your father's case…. forget it. Quite frankly, I was never completely convinced that it was your father that did those bombings."

Fred had his drink glass halfway to his lips when he stopped………

"What? What makes you say that?" He put his drink back down without tasting it. Roy shuffled in his chair a bit before he spoke.

"Look Fred, you were in charge of that case. When it was over, you appeared to be satisfied that it was solved. But, after you left, I thought a lot about it. Things didn't totally add up for me."

"Like what?"

"Well, for one thing, your father. He just didn't seem to be the type for violence. Even with his history connecting him with that Ann Harbor SDS group. He was anti-war, ya, but his persona was different." Roy leaned back in his chair, threw an arm over the chair and ran his finger around the rim of his drink glass. "Another thing is, when we found him at the post office the night he died, the bag he was carrying was empty."

Fred looked at him, "So?"

"I thought, who carries an empty bag? I mean if you're planting a bomb, wouldn't you have extra pieces of wire, wire clippers, tape, that sort of thing. Not an empty bag."

"Roy, maybe he just carried the bomb there."

"Perhaps, but if I were gonna bomb a place, I'd make sure I had stuff to connect the bomb. I mean, I surely wouldn't carry an active bomb in my car. Hell no, I'd wait till I got to the place I was gonna denotate it. Then I'd use the wires, wire cutters, and tape to activate it. Anyway, that's how I thought it out. Nope, he just didn't seem to be the type."

Fred was rubbing his forehead, processing what Roy had just said, then he looked up quickly. "Then why the hell was he there?"

Roy just shook his head while he continued to run his finger around the glass rim. "Don't know. However, if you're not carrying something to a site, then perhaps you're carrying something away. One or the other."

"Roy, you think he was there to pick up the bomb? But why?"

"Again, I don't know Fred. Who else had a motive to plant a bomb? But it's a done deal now, the case is closed. But I'll tell ya this, Police Chief Harrison kept asking me questions about those bombings long after you had left for California."

"Harrison? But why?" Roy had stopped playing with his drink glass and took a sip.

"Sorry Fred, I have no answers for you. Maybe he was just tidying up loose ends for his report. Or maybe he had some other ideas about the bombings. I just don't know."

Fred looked around the room thinking about what Roy said. If you're not carrying something to a place, then perhaps you're gonna carry something away. But no one walks around with an empty bag.

It was nine o'clock when Fred and Roy left the VFW. Roy had to work the next day, so Fred went back to the Hilton. When he got into his room, the red button on the phone was blinking. He picked it up and got a voice message from Allie. She wanted to meet him for dinner at her place the following night. He hung up and wrote a brief note for himself on the hotel note pad about the dinner. Then he poured a glass of Jameson and sat in a chair looking out over the Minneapolis night skyline. His conversation with Roy was swirling around in his head. Why did his father have an empty bag? He decided that tomorrow he'd try and contact Chief Police Harrison. He put down his glass of drink, walked over and laid on the bed, and fell right to sleep.

CHAPTER 22

After she hung up the phone, Allie wondered if she did the right thing, calling Fred like that for dinner. She thought it might appear she was chasing after him. Would she look desperate? She liked Fred, and after their rendezvous in his room, was she expecting him to fall all over her? The guy didn't seem to be all that anxious to call her. Maybe he was distracted dealing with his mother. Perhaps he had things on his mind and would have called eventually. Allie thought that Fred, like many guys, was slow at picking up on subtle hints. After all, he always seemed to be interested in her. Even when they worked together, there was the hint of sexual tension. A little flirtatious bantering was present at times. However, she knew that any involvement with another employee was never a good thing. She felt he had the same thought, and that's why during the five years they worked together, nothing happened. She walked over to the kitchen counter to her wine glass, took a sip, and pursed her lips in thought. Could she very well be overthinking this? Taking her wine glass, she went over to the couch and sat down. She grabbed the CD remote player, and turned-on the smooth jazz sound of saxophonist Gato Barbieri. Laying her head back against the head rest, she thought about that night in Fred's room. Allie enjoyed it, she enjoyed his company, and his presence, Hell, she enjoyed everything about that night. To her, Fred was the right blend of personalities. He was on a good career path. People liked being around him, he made them feel comfortable. The guy was very respectful of people. He treated the mail handlers and postal clerks the same way he did those in upper management. Of course, it didn't hurt that he was good to look at. Allie knew she was almost thirty-five and that perhaps should be looking for a serious relationship.

In her life Allie had two, what some might call, serious relationships. One was a guy in college who wanted to be a doctor. She soon realized that most things were about him, there was way too much giving and too little getting. In their junior year, she broke it off. Allie could not view any future with someone who always had to be the center of attention. The second relationship was a few years out of college. She was introduced to a corporate lawyer who worked on the top floor of the IDS tower in Minneapolis. They hit it right off. He and Allie seemed to be made for each other. Their interests in travel, shows, and outdoor activities were similar. That relationship all came to an end when he started to drink more. Allie sensed that his work demands were getting the best of him, so he drank to relax. That wouldn't have been so bad except he got belligerent after a few drinks. He'd start an argument over small things, questioned her decisions, made unfavorable comments on clothes she wore. Even a sit-down heart to heart talk with him didn't help. The final straw was when he almost got into a fight at 'The Local', one of their favorite restaurants. He had been drinking and made a remark to a couple at another table. Things got heated to a point where the servers had to intervene. Allie was so embarrassed that she just grabbed her purse and walked out. She never answered his phone calls, never saw him again. After that, she just dated from time to time, deciding to enjoy life and see what comes. Life was good. Allie had her own townhouse, a good job, and great girlfriends. But like many things, there was a void, she knew it, and realized that at some point she'd want to contemplate the possibility of another relationship.

When she started to work for Fred, she thought, perhaps it could work with a guy like that. However, she knew it would never happen. Office romances rarely worked out, and if it did, the working environment changed. When Fred left his position for a new life, she thought that perhaps she should do the same. However, time changes people's ideas about shifting their lifestyle. No, for now, Allie decided to stay put and work on improving her career.

Allie realized her wine glass was empty and the CD was replaying itself.
It was getting late, and she felt tired, or maybe it was the wine. She
turned the CD player off, walked over, and put the wine glass in the
sink. She went back into the living room to close the drapes but
stopped. She looked out over the Minneapolis lights and thought, I
like that man. I wonder if he likes me the same. She closed the drapes
and went to bed.

Mid-day, Allie received a call from Fred. They agreed upon a six-thirty
dinner time, and he was going to bring some wine. The phone call
brightened her day. She had something to look forward to that didn't
involve her girlfriends. Allie couldn't remember the last time she had
an actual date. She had been asked out for dates before, but the men
who asked were not her type. She felt it would be wrong to go out
with a guy she wasn't interested in. Her thought was, why waste a
guy's time if you didn't want to be with him. She walked into her
closet and picked a nice, casual outfit, pants, and a matching top. She
put on her shoes, grabbed her car keys, and drove over to Byerly's off
highway 494 in Minneapolis. She parked her vehicle, and went in.
Byerly's was one of her favorite stores to shop. It had so many
different types of groceries and specialty items. Grabbing a grocery
cart, she made her way around the glass enclosed meat counters. The
selection would make any would-be cook dizzy with the various
selections. She had her eye on some Boar's Head Ham that she could
almost taste just standing there. There was also a variety of prepared
salads that would go great with the ham.
"May I help you ma'am?" The sudden voice caught Allie off guard.
She had to look around to see where it came from. Then she noticed a
short clerk behind the counter wearing a white apron, and a small hat
with the store's name on it.
"Ahh, not right now, I'm just browsing." Allie could not make up her
mind what to get. She really didn't know what to do for dinner.
Mainly, she didn't know what Fred liked. She wandered Byerly's
picking up a few essentials and then decided to make a favorite

Minnesota go-to dish for Fred. She walked by the flower section and decided to get an arrangement for the table. Allie wondered if guys really paid attention to flowers on a table, did they really care? What the hell, she thought, and threw the flowers in her cart. The rest of the day was spent doing errands before she headed back to her townhouse in the Lowry Hill section of St. Paul. The day went fast, and Allie felt she needed to get in gear if she wanted to be ready when Fred came. A nice bubble bath would put her in a good frame of mind to meet him. Before she drew her bath, she prepared the night's dinner. It would be ready to cook when the time came. For some unknown reason, Allie felt a bit nervous. She couldn't tell if it was because she wanted tonight to go well, or the fact that it had been quite a while since she last entertained a guy. She finally thought, what the hell just go for it and let fate work out the details. With her new mind set, she headed to take her bath.

It was slightly before six thirty when Fred arrived. After parking his rental car, he walked up to Allie's townhouse on Summit Avenue. When she answered the door, Fred gave a short low whistle.
"Wow, you look stunning." Allie could feel a sophomoric blush in her face. She laughed.
"Well, I didn't see that coming." Fred reached out, took her hand, and spun her around, admiring her. She was dressed in a simple short black dress that outlined her best features.
"Seriously Allie, you make that dress envious of you. I don't know fashion, but I'd say you nailed it."
"C'mon Fred, it's a simple black dress, you're making too much of it."
"It may be a dress, but you make it look more than simple."
She put her hand on his shoulder and gently guided him inside.
"Oh, get in here before the neighbors think you're a bill collector."
Fred walked in and looked around. "You have a really nice place. How long have you lived here?" He went over to the kitchen and placed a bottle of Malbec wine on the counter.
"Guess it's going on six years since I moved in. I was going to buy a

house, but I'm not a good one for repairs or working in the yard. I thought a townhouse would do just right for me." Allie went into the kitchen and turned the oven on.

"It'll be forty minutes or so before dinner is ready. Would you like a drink?"

"Sure, what ya got?"

"I think I may have some Jameson, if you're interested?"

"Oh, you're a woman after my own heart."

Allie thought, he's not far off. She poured him a drink and made a vodka tonic for herself.

"Let's sit in the living room while we wait." They walked over and sat on the couch. During the day when she cleaned the house, Allie arranged the furniture so they would both sit on the couch. Afterall it was a date, and she didn't want him to be sitting across from her. She turned to him. "So, how'd your day go? What did you do to occupy your time?"

He took a sip of his drink and said, "Sadly, I worked. Needed to know what's going on in my absence. Plus, there were a few loose ends I had to take care of. I didn't want to go back and find a mess. I mean, I have confidence in the people I work with, but I feel out of the loop." They talked about the past, people they knew, and some idle chit chat before the oven timer went off.

"Looks like dinner's ready." Allie put her empty glass on the coffee table and went into the kitchen. "Why don't you go over to the table and sit down, I'll bring the food." Fred uncorked the bottle, poured the wine, and looked up. Allie was standing there with a smile and tonight's dinner. She spoke, "Look mister, I wasn't sure what to make for dinner and I'm not much of a cook." With a smile she said, "But what better way to say welcome back than a good old Minnesota Tater Tot hotdish."

Fred slapped the table with both hands, leaned back, and gave a short laugh. That's fantastic! I haven't had Tater Tot hotdish in ages." He had a gentle smile, "It really is perfect, good comfort food. Thank you,

Allie." She put the hotdish on the table and served up a portion for each.

The rest of the evening went pretty much as before dinner, good conversation and reminiscing about the past. Allie's suspicion about the flowers was right. He didn't even notice them. After eating, they moved back into the living room. Fred had another Jameson, and Allie still had her wine glass from dinner. There was smooth music on the CD player as the evening wore on. Somewhere in their conversation they found themselves sitting closer together. Neither could remember how it happened but neither thought more about it. At some point, Fred was aware of the faint scent of Allie's perfume. It was ever so subtle, just a hint, a tease, enough to weaken a man's resolve. While Allie was talking, he looked at her lips moving. He remembered how soft they were the last time he kissed her. He noticed she had stopped talking and was looking at him.
"You OK Fred? You're looking a bit strange."
He smiled, "No I'm good. I was just looking at your lips."
She smiled, put her glass down. "And?"
He gently pulled her closer and kissed her. It was just like before, soft, warm, and inviting. The music and drinks had their effect. They sat there for a short period, kissing, when she spoke.
"Perhaps we should get more comfortable." They got up, and went into her bedroom, slowly undressing each other while kissing. They laid down and enjoyed the feeling of skin on skin. The gentle touches, the soft kisses on her fingertips, and shoulders. He felt as if he was dining on her skin. The love making, starting slowly, built up like an ocean wave, reached a pinnacle, and then tumbled over itself, slowly ebbing, to where their hearts beat heavily, and their breathing was quick and shallow. They laid there, physically, and emotionally exhausted. He turned his head slowly towards her, and in a low, husky, breathless voice he said. "You're incredible! You've used up any strength that I had. Making love to you is magnificent."
Allie put an arm on her forehead, and in a low, soft breath said, "You

had my total attention and more. I don't know where you got the energy, but wow." After lying there for a while, their breathing returned to normal. He placed his arm under her head. She rolled gently towards him, put her arm over his chest, and they both fell asleep.

The sun was shining directly in Fred's face when he woke. He put a hand up to block the sun. He squinted a few times to adjust his eyes to the morning light. Allie murmured a little and snuggled closer. "Morning sunshine." She murmured again. He smiled. "I know you can hear me." She made a playful grunt, indicating she didn't want to be awake. "C'mon, I'm not gonna be awake by myself." She made another small grunt and turned over, taking more of the sheet with her. He turned towards her. "You have any coffee?" Allie, without moving, raised an arm, pointing behind them towards the kitchen and went, "mmmm." He was still smiling and thought she was cute in the morning. He got up and sat on the side of the bed, gave a big yawn, and scratched his backside. After putting on his trousers, he walked into the kitchen and found the Mr. Coffee and coffee makings. Within fifteen minutes, he was back at the bed on Allie's side. He placed her cup of coffee on the nightstand.

"Wake up sleepyhead, I've got coffee." Those must have been the magic words because she immediately rolled over, wrinkled her brow, and squinted.

"It's too bright," she pulled the sheet over her head. He reached over and pulled it back off.

"C'mon, I have some coffee here for you." She opened her eyes and gave a muffled yawn with her hand.

"What time is it?"

"It's eight-thirty and looks like a beautiful day."

"Oh God!" She rolled over and pulled the sheets back over her head.

"C'mon Allie, don't let me drink coffee alone." She rolled back over, sat up, blinked, and stretched. He handed her the coffee.

"Mmmm, nothing tastes so great as that first cup of coffee in the

morning." She smiled at him. Do you always get up so early?"
He took a sip of coffee. "Sometimes I do, sometimes I don't, but I
don't consider this early."
She looked at him. "When you're on vacation it is."
"Well, I'm not on vacation, remember?"
"Yaaaa," she said as she yawned. "So, what are your plans today,
anything special?"
"First, I have to check in with my mother to see how she is doing. Then
I'd like to contact Chief of Police Harrison. There are a few things I'd
like to talk about with him."
"The bombing?" Allie said.
"Ya, the bombings. After this coffee, I'm heading back to the hotel to
shower, shave, and put on some fresh clothes. So, get your butt going
so we can both start the day."
Finishing their coffee, Allie got out of bed and Fred got dressed. She
walked over to him wearing a bathrobe and leaned against him.
"Last night was nice, thank you." She kissed him.
"I should be thanking you. The whole evening was great, and the Tater
Tot dish was a nice touch. And the dessert was spectacular." He
kissed her back. She walked him to the door and gave him one more
kiss. "I'll call you later Allie." She smiled, watching him walk to his car.
I definitely like that man, she thought. She closed the door and
headed to the shower.

CHAPTER 23

Fred was looking for his car keys as he prepared to leave the Hilton. He had showered, shaved and put fresh clothes on. It was a great night with Allie, and he felt refreshed. It surprised him how easy it was to be with her. They got along great and seemed to have a passion for each other. He also wondered if it was just an infatuation or the real thing. Fred was in Minnesota to visit his mother, anything beyond that was extra. He didn't want to think that his time with Allie was just a fling. He really liked the woman, but perhaps it was the wrong time. With keys in hand, he was out the door.

It was over a half hour before he arrived at his mother's house. He parked in the driveway and entered the house through the kitchen door. Not seeing her in the kitchen he yelled out.

"Mom!" He faintly heard a voice upstairs. Walking over to the foot of the staircase, he yelled again. "Mom!" At the top of the stairs, she smiled down at him.

"Up here, Fred. My goodness, didn't you hear me answer the first time?"

"Well, kinda. I thought I heard a voice, but I wasn't sure."

"Who do you think was answering, the boogeyman?" She slowly started to make her way down.

"Be careful, Mom."

"Oh, for God's sake Fred, I've been up and down these stairs for over forty years, another year is not going to make a difference."

Again, he was amazed at her resilience. It kept him in awe of her ability. He felt he really didn't know this woman. She had raised three sons, made a home for them and their father, but Fred never gave thought to the inner woman. At the bottom of the stairs, she brushed a loose strand of hair off her forehead. She straightened up, leaned over and kissed him, then they walked toward the kitchen.

"So, how was your night? You go anywhere?" She put the tea kettle on the stove and sat down.

"Oh, I just had dinner with a friend." He walked over and sat down across from her. "How are you feeling, Mom?" He put his elbows on the table and leaned towards her. "Did you sleep well last night?"

"Slept really good. Had a dream about your father," a pleasant look came over her face. "We were at Mac's restaurant, and he was singing a song to everyone. I don't know what that was all about." She reached over smiling and touched his arm. "I mean you know how dreams are weird. Especially this one, because your father couldn't sing if his life depended on it." She leaned back and had a pleasant look on her face. "I do miss that man." She took a napkin out of her apron and wiped her nose. The tea kettle whistled. "How about some nice tea?"

"Sure Mom, sure." Fred realized his Mom was living in two worlds, the present and the past. Perhaps as you get older that is what life gives you, a taste of the old and a taste of the new. Life balances things out to let you choose where you want to spend your time. When an older person is seen staring out the window, they are choosing to be in the past world. A world of memories, some good, some not so good, but it's a familiar world. It's unlike the present one where old friends are long gone and things are changing fast.

His mother came back with the tea and poured a cup for each of them. "Say Mom, did John stay long last night?"

"Oh, we watched TV for a while, then he went to the basement. Said he wanted to clean up some more. I must have fallen I asleep in the chair because he woke me later and asked if I wanted to go to bed. She looked at Fred, "Isn't it strange that people will wake you up and ask if you want to go to sleep." Fred smiled. "Anyway, I went upstairs and went to bed. I thought John was going to stay, but he's been away from his house so long I bet he needed to take care of a few things." Fred stirred the tea bag in his cup, "So John was in the basement, huh?"

"Yes, he's been carrying things out every day. I'd be surprised if there is anything left."

"Mom, I'm gonna check it out, there may be a few things I could help with." Fred got up and made his way into the basement. He detected the same scent as before, only this time it was a bit stronger. He saw the two cardboard boxes still on the worktable. Beside them were pieces of cut wire and black tape. Fred looked into the boxes and saw electronic parts. He didn't know his father was into electronics, but then again there was a lot he didn't know about him. He was about to leave when he saw a store receipt on the floor. He picked it up and saw it was from Best Buy. His eyes looked at the date, three weeks ago. Fred wondered why there would be a receipt from three weeks ago if John was taking things out. He went back upstairs.

"Mom, did John say when he'd be back?

"Not really. He does check in with me at different times during the day." He put the receipt in his pocket.

"Mom, I have a few things to do today, would you mind if I just checked in with you later?"

"Sure Fred, take care of your things, and maybe your friend...?" He smiled at her.

"Thanks for the tea, Mom." Fred left and headed to see Chief of Police Harrison.

It was slightly past two o'clock when Fred arrived at the St. Paul police station on Grove Street. At the front desk he asked for Chief Harrison's office. He took the stairs up, turned right, found the office, and went inside. A young receptionist looked up.

"May I help you sir?"

"Ah ya, is the Chief in?"

"Yes, he is, may I say who's calling?"

"Cosman, Fred Cosman."

The young woman got on the phone. "Sir, there is a gentleman out here wishing to see you." There was a slight pause. "A Mr. Cosman, sir. Yes, ok. Mr. Cosman you can go right in."

Fred found Harrison sitting behind a large, old style oak desk. Papers of all type covered the top. The Chief got up and extended his hand. "Hello, Fred. Good to see you. I heard you were in town and was hoping to visit with you at some point." Fred shook the Chief's hand and sat down.

"How'd ya know I was in town?"

"Your former colleague Inspector Downing called and gave me a heads up. He knew I was interested in contacting you."

"Really, what'd ya want to see me about?" Fred leaned back in his chair.

"Oh, it can wait. I don't suspect that you came all the way down here just to visit with me. What did you have in mind?"

"Well, look Chief."

"It's Pat. You can call me Pat. Chief sounds so formal." He moved some papers aside as to indicate he was giving Fred his full attention.

"Umm, Chief, err Pat, it's like this. I am watching the news the other night about a bombing at the post office. Naturally, it piqued my interests, and I was wondering if it had anything to do with the previous bombings, we were all investigating. I realize this might be a big imposition, but I thought you could help me resolve my suspicions. It might be a lot to ask but, well, you can understand my curiosity." The Chief leaned back in his chair and tapped a pencil on the edge of his desk.

"Yes, well that was actually what I wanted to discuss with you." He looked at Fred. "With what little you know about the recent bombing; would you say it look remarkably close to the case we worked on? I mean, as best as you know, does it appear to be a coincidence?"

"Actually, it does. That's why I wanted to see you. Wanted to know your thoughts on it." The Chief stopped tapping the pencil and looked down at it. Then he spoke.

"Ya know Fred, I'm old school. When I worked at the NYPD and had a case, even though I might have a case solved, I always viewed every piece of evidence. Sometimes cases were solved without viewing all the evidence. It could be that easy. However, an old timer once told me that many times evidence can lead you astray. That unless you looked at everything, it wasn't solved. Simply put, never go for the quick fix. The last piece of evidence looked at could turn a case around. It all must fit from the beginning to the end. That's where I find myself now." He looked at Fred. "You know what I'm saying?" Fred looked puzzled.

"You, talking about the recent bombing?"

"No, I am talking about the bombings your father was allegedly involved in."

Fred's eyes got wide. He moved to the edge of his chair and put one hand on Harrison's desk. "You said allegedly. Are you suggesting that my father wasn't setting off those bombs?"

"No, I'm saying that all the pieces, the evidence, has to fit. And for me, it didn't." The Chief got up, went to a filing cabinet and took out a folder, came back and sat down. He put the folder in front of him and opened it. He flipped through a few pages and pulled out one sheet. "After your Dad passed away, everyone thought the case was closed. Now, I mentioned I'm old school, so I wanted to view all the evidence, not just the obvious. I sent the bag he was carrying to the FBI forensic lab for testing. I wanted to tie up all loose ends." He handed the paper he was holding to Fred. "As you can see, there was no evidence of residue of a bomb. Not a scent of powder, no hint of anything remotely connected to a bomb." Fred was looking over the paper. "You know what they did find?" Fred stopped reading and looked up intently. "They found wood chips. Very small wood chips. It looks as if someone was carrying wood in that bag." Fred sat there thinking back to when he was young. He remembered his father going out to a wood pile to bring wood back to their fireplace. He couldn't totally remember what the bag looked like, but he knew it had two handles, one on each side.

"You're telling me that only thing that was carried in that bag was wood?"

"No." The Chief paused. "There may have been other things, but what it didn't carry was a bomb. So, I don't know what your father was using that bag for, but there was no evidence of a bomb."

"That's it? That's all your suspicions? I mean he could have had a bomb wrapped in something." Fred didn't know what to make of this. First Roy brings up the bag and now the Chief. He needed more to hang his hopes on than a damn bag.

"No, that's not all Fred. I asked Agent James if he could have the FBI do a profile check on your father. Many times, certain types of people perform various crimes. The FBI is good at it."

Fred challenged the Chief. "So is my father the type or not?"

"Not. First of all, old men do not resort to bombing. It's not their MO. They may use guns, poison, run you over with a car, but not bombing. He's not the type." Fred looked to one side, he was slightly confused, if it wasn't his father, then who? He turned back to the Chief.

"Ok, what type fits the mold of a bomber?"

The Chief pulled out another paper from the folder and held it. "Do you remember Ted Kaczynski?"

Fred nodded, "Ya, the Unabomber. He set off a few bombs back in the seventies."

"I'm impressed, many people your age wouldn't know that."

"Well, they went over him at the Academy when I was there. He sent the bombs through the mail, so the Academy used him as an example of what we might expect. Besides, what's he got to do with this?"

He's the type to send bombs. His profile was, a young Caucasian, say between thirty and forty years of age, intelligent, and someone who had a beef with the establishment. Mainly a government agency of any type, military, academic, even a post office. That's the kind of person that sets off bombs. Not an old man. Besides, your father was too set in his ways to change. And certainly not agile enough to be running around at night hopping on and off postal docks. I mean the guy had arthritis. Like I said, you have to look at all the evidence before coming to a conclusion. Too many people have been convicted because they were at the wrong place at the wrong time. And they were convicted with just some of the evidence." He handed the paper he was holding to Fred. He looked it over slowly.

"What you have in your hand describes exactly what I said. That's who we should have been looking for. And that's who we think set off this latest bomb. The guy is still out there Fred, and I'm gonna get him."

Fred left the Chief's office in a daze. He thought, my father didn't set off those bombs, yet he got blamed for it. Was he in the wrong place at the wrong time for the wrong reason? Then why the hell was he there? Could Roy be right, that Dad was there to retrieve the bombs? But if he was, why? Why was he retrieving the bomb, and how did he know about it? The argument that John and their father had, did they both know who was doing it. Was John yelling at his father not to get involved? The more he thought about it the more questions he had. It was five o'clock, he told his mother he'd be back, but he needed a drink. He called Allie instead and asked if she'd meet him at the VFW. He needed someone to talk to. They agreed to meet in a half hour.

Allie found Fred in a back booth. He already had one empty glass in front of him. She slid in beside him.

"Kind of anxious, are we?" He half smiled. A waitress came over and took Allie's drink order.

"I don't know, Allie. I got a lot to think about." The waitress came back with a drink. Fred proceeded to fill Allie in about his conversation with Chief Harrison. He went over what the Chief suspected. He also explained about the forensic results of the bag and the bomber profile. She sat there intently listening to him. She spoke up.

"So, the Chief doesn't think it was your father?"

"Well, that's what he implied, and he backed it up with evidence." Fred went on to explain about the Chief's old school approach that led him to his convictions.

"But that's good, isn't it?" Allie said. "I mean it will clear your father. Right?"

"Afraid not Allie. What we have is the beginning of a new case. What has to be shown is who planted those bombs, and are they tied in with this latest one. No Allie. This is just the beginning.

They finished their drinks and went back to Allie's townhouse. This night, the love making was more intense, it was exceeded by their desires. They would lay there exhausted, but eventually the passion was ignited again. Neither could explain their hunger for each other. Perhaps it was pent up emotions from years of working together but unable to do anything about it. But it was just two individuals, whose desire for each other was finally consummated. A fiery passion that culminated in their love making. Exhausted and with energy spent, they both fell asleep.

CHAPTER 24

It was noon the next day when Fred arrived at his mother's house. He saw that John's pickup was already in the driveway. This is going to be interesting he thought. He hadn't seen his brother in a few days and had some questions for him. Entering through the kitchen door, he saw his mother.

"Hi Mom. How are you feeling today?"

His mother had just put the smoked shoulder in the oven and was closing the door.

"Hi son." She brushed that one strand of hair away from her forehead. "I'm doing good, not tired at all. It feels good to be busy. You know what they say about idle hands." She wiped her hands on her apron and walked over to the kitchen table.

"Where's John mom? I see his truck out there."

"I believe he's watching TV, or down in the basement. I swear he's becoming more like your father. Always going to the…. what do you call it? Oh yes, the man cave. You men really have a way of describing places you like to escape to."

Fred's brow furled, he looked at this as an Aha, moment. Whatever John was doing down there, this was Fred's chance to catch him at it. He went to the door and descended the stair quickly. John was at the table sorting through the cardboard boxes. He turned when he heard the noise behind him.

"Hey sport, finally decided to show up?" He turned back around to the boxes.

This annoyed Fred. "What do you mean by that? Mom invited both of us for dinner."

John kept busy with the boxes. Then he said, "Ya, but where were you Friday night? I thought you were coming back to be with Mom."

Fred was caught a bit off guard by John's question. He knew he had no real good reason. "I had a meeting and it got late; I knew you were coming over." Fred found himself lying. "I needed to wash up and change clothes, and I just fell asleep."

His brother turned to him and sarcastically said, "It's good you get your rest, this trip must be wearing you out." Fred decided to let the comment pass.

"What're ya working on there?" He pointed to the cardboard boxes and tools.

"Just sorting out stuff Dad had." Fred pulled the store receipt out of his pocket.

"You working on new stuff? I found this receipt on the floor the other day." Fred thought this was the moment where John couldn't explain it. His brother took the receipt and looked at it.

"Oh ya, I brought some batteries for the smoke detector and carbon monoxide alarm. I don't think Dad ever changed the batteries when they died."

Fred pushed the issue, "What about the tape and wire purchases?" He thought he had John.

"Ya, well the smoke alarm was hard wired into the house system. The batteries were back up, in case of failure, but the wiring was frayed, and I fixed them. That answer your questions, Inspector?"

Fred felt he was on thin ice with his question. "What's that funky scent down here?"

John shrugged his shoulders, "I don't smell anything, maybe it was the cleaning solution I used to clean up this place by myself." John turned and stared at him. "Anything else Sherlock?"

Fred could feel the frustration building up inside him. He rubbed his forehead. "Why do you have to be so confrontational?" I ask you a few questions and you get an attitude." Fred stared at him.

John looked right back at him. "You come over here under the pretense of a Sunday dinner and start questioning me like I was being investigated. I mean, who the hell do you think you are? What gives you the right to be questioning me? My attitude is the direct result of your interrogation." John turned back around and faced the workbench.

Fred realized he wasn't handling this well. He had some questions but understood how his brother could take offense.

"Look John, I just had some questions. You seem to disappear, acting kinda mysterious and all. Mom says you've been spending a lot of time down here. I see the electronics parts, tape, and wire. I was just wondering what you were doing." By now, Fred didn't want to pursue his suspicions about the wire and electronic parts. He needed more information, and he didn't know where to get it. He turned around and went upstairs.

The rest of the afternoon was awkward. The Cosman family ate their Sunday dinner, somewhat in silence. The brothers didn't have much to say. If they said anything, it was directed to their mother. After dinner, their mother spent her time in the kitchen cleaning up. Fred helped wipe the dishes while John worked in the backyard. His mother put the last of the dishes away and asked Fred to sit down. "Fred, what's going on between you and your brother? You two hardly spoke to one another at dinner. Both of you spoke to me but not really to each other."

"I don't know, Mom. I am finding it hard to talk with John. He seems so touchy." His mother took the handkerchief out of her apron and twirled it in her hands.

"Does it have anything to do with the bomb that went off at the post office?" She was looking down at her hands.

Fred got a strange look on his face. "Why would you say that Mom?"

"Son, you may just see me as your mother, but I'm not dumb. This family has an odd association with bombs in the past. What your father did or did not do, hangs on this family like a plague. I just thought that, since you had investigated those other bombings perhaps you were doing it again. Unofficially, of course. I thought that's what's causing you and John to have differences."

Fred sat there amazed. He really didn't know his mother. She did all the motherly things but appeared to have no interests in things beyond her small world. However, her perception about the bombings was incredible. He had to remind himself that she was a college graduate. She was a smart woman yet kept things to herself. Like the Cheshire Cat, in Alice in Wonderland, she watched and took things in. "Well, I did watch the latest bombing on the news the other day, and it brought back a lot of questions."

His mother looked straight at him. "So, do you think this family is involved again?"

Listening to her, Fred thought, there's that woman again. The woman who sat there the night his father died. The stoic, strong person asking all the right questions.   "I don't know how, Mom. Quite frankly, I'm beginning to think Dad wasn't responsible for those previous bombings. I know he and John had an argument before we found Dad at the post office that night. How that tie in, I don't know?"

"So, you think your father wasn't involved? How did you come by that conclusion?"

Fred moved uncomfortably in his chair. "I spoke with Chief of Police Harrison on Friday. He's been revisiting the evidence on that case." Fred tried to be evasive so he wouldn't give his mother false hope. "Nothing specific. He just mentioned he had unanswered questions."

"Son, tell me. Is that what you and your brother are in disagreement about? I feel that he still blames the post office, for not only Joey's death, but your father's as well. Whatever it is Fred, I need you to be honest with me. If you find something out that affects this family, I need to know."

"I will Mom, I will."

John walked in through the kitchen door. "Well Mom, I got the backyard cleaned up. All the tools put away. Your flowers are gonna look really good this year."

"Thanks John, I appreciate it. I'm finding it harder to get up and down at the flower bed. The old grey mare isn't what she used to be." She gave him a smile.

"Say Mom, if it's OK, I'm gonna take off now. I have things to do at my place."

"Of course, son. Thanks for the yard work, and don't forget the Tupperware on the counter. I made you up some leftovers."

John kissed his mother goodbye and looked over at Fred. "Take it easy, sport." He walked out.

Fred went over to the kitchen widow and looked out. He saw his brother get in his truck with the Tupperware and another box. He went down into the basement and saw just one cardboard box. Plus, the tape, wires, and tools were gone. Fred knew he had to speak with Inspector Roy Downing again. He kissed his mother goodbye and headed back to the Hilton.

CHAPTER 25

His cell phone rang four times before Fred reached for it. In the dark, he knocked it off the end table.

"Damn it!" He reached over, ran his hand around the floor till he found it.

"Ahhlo?"

"Fred?"

"Ahhlo?"

"Fred!"

"Whoo's this?"

"Fred, it's me, Roy Downing."

"What time is it?" Fred rubbed his eyes with his hands.

"It's two-thirty. Fred, wake up."

"Two-thirty?" Why the hell are you calling me at this hour?"

"Fred, there was another bombing." He immediately became awake and sat up in the bed."

"Whaaat?"

"There's been another bombing. This time it's at the Minneapolis post office dock."

"Another bombing? When? Fred pushed the bed covers off him, turned and sat at the edge of the bed.

"About forty-five minutes ago."

"Anybody hurt?"

"A maintenance guy. He has some bruises and is pretty shook up. Other than that, he seems OK."

"Why are you calling me?"

"Well, the maintenance man gave a brief description of a guy he saw running from the dock. I think you might want to come down. Chief Harrison is here also."

"Harrison? Isn't that out of his jurisdiction? I mean it's Minneapolis, not St. Paul."

"I know, but the situation seemed to warrant calling him. The similarities of the bombing are too close to the case we worked on over a year ago. Can you come down?"

"Give me a half hour or so." Fred hung up the phone, got dressed, grabbed his keys, and was out the door.

He pulled into the postal parking lot and stopped over by the ambulance. He immediately saw Roy and walked over.

"Morning Fred, sorry to bring you out on this."

With a whimsical look Fred said, "Ya, good morning."

Roy reached into his vehicle and handed Fred a cup of coffee. "I thought you could use this." Fred took the coffee, pulled the top off, and took a sip.

"Ahhh, that tastes good. So, what do we have here?" Fred was looking over at the ambulance, the dock, and the police cars.

Roy spoke up, "Well, around quarter of two, the maintenance guy was making his way to the end of the dock. He said he heard a noise and the next thing he knew he was on his ass. The explosion came from one of the mailbags unloaded earlier. Thank God the mail handlers were on their lunch break. Most of the explosion was at the end of the dock, so the rest of it was not damaged." Just as he finished, Chief Harrison walked up.

"Morning Fred."

Fred had a smirk, "Ya, good morning."

"Sorry to involve you in this, but we thought you could help us."

He looked at the Chief, "Help you? How the hell am I supposed to be of any help? I'm just visiting here." He took another sip of his coffee.

"I know Fred, but the similarities of this bombing are too close to the ones a year ago. We, that is Roy and I, thought that the three of us can pool our memories. Come up with a possible scenario."

Fred looked at the two of them. "It's a bombing, maybe a copycat, but it's a bombing. You eliminate what ya know and the 'who done it' will show up. What about this guy the maintenance man said he saw?"

"Well, that's part of why we called you. Because of your knowledge and familiarity with the previous case."

Fred looked first at Roy and then at the Chief. "I don't get it, what's this got to do with me."

The Chief spoke, "The description the maintenance man gave was, a guy, in his late thirties maybe early forties, slender to medium build."

Fred slowly shook his head, shrugged his shoulders, and smiled. "Well, that solves it, you just described half the young men in Minneapolis."

Roy put his hand on Fred's shoulder, "The guy drove away in a pickup."

Fred got an uneasy feeling in his stomach, "What color?"

"It was a dark color, maybe black, maybe blue, could be a dark green," the Chief said.

Fred spoke, "So, what we have here is a guy, thirty to forty, slender to medium built, driving away in a dark pickup. And this was witnessed by an old guy at night? I would say that information is pretty slim." Fred threw the remainder of his coffee on the ground. "Sorry gents, but from where I stand, you have information that describes half the guys and pickup trucks in this city. It says nothing."

Roy and the Chief looked at one another. The Chief said, "Look, we're all tired. Could we meet tomorrow in my office around one o'clock? That'll give us time to go home, get something to eat, and get some sleep. We'll be more refreshed." Roy nodded approval.

"I still don't see what this has got to do with me. I'm an outsider." Fred said.

Chief Harrison looked at him. "Look Fred. You have knowledge and experience in these cases. Besides I have some information I'd like you to look at. Information you might find interesting. I…. that is, we, need your help."

Fred felt he couldn't refuse. He stifled a yawn and said, "OK, OK, we meet tomorrow, one o'clock in your office." He walked to his vehicle and drove off.

On the drive back to the Hilton, Fred pondered why the Chief and Roy were so adamant in getting him involved. He thought he was done with this part of his life. But events seem to be drawing him back in.

The description of the mysterious guy the maintenance man saw bothered Fred. A thirty- to forty-year-old guy, slender to medium build, driving a dark colored pickup. He hated to admit it, but it described his brother John, almost. It was dark and the maintenance guy could be mistaken. Half of all eyewitnesses get details wrong. Three different people will come up with three different descriptions of a suspect. Fred thought of the irony, he…. found himself in. The same scenario that resulted in his leaving the postal service. Fate seemed to be testing him, seeing how he'd handle it this time. He yawned as he pulled into the Hilton parking lot. He went upstairs, entered his room throwing the keys on the end table. Taking off only his shoes, he crawled into bed and fell right to sleep.

It was slightly past one o'clock when Fred arrived at Chief Harrison's office. Roy and the Chief were already there.

"Afternoon Fred, grab yourself a cup of coffee. Roy and I were just going over the events of last night, or this morning, I guess. For some reason, it seems more appropriate to call it last night." Roy looked up at Fred and said hi. Fred poured a cup of coffee and sat across from the Chief.

"So, what do we have here? Anything new?" He took a sip of his coffee.

Harrison looked at him. "Not much from last night. I sent off pieces of the bomb and anything associated with it to the FBI forensic lab. We should have something back in a week."

"A week? You don't think I'm gonna stay around here for a week?" Fred slid forward in his chair. "Pat, look, this is not my job. In a week I'll be out in sunny California, doing what I get paid for."

The Chief came around Fred's side and sat on the corner of the desk. "We know Fred. We didn't expect you to work on this case or stay around."

"Then why in the hell am I here?"

The Chief reached over and picked up a folder from his desk.

"Remember last night when I said I had information you might find interesting?" He handed the folder to Fred. "What you have there is the combined information from the bombing a year back, and recent information from a few days ago." Fred opened the folder and leafed through the pages. The Chief continued, "At the time during the first bombing case, one of our officers picked up three young guys in a vehicle. You remember that?" Without looking up, Fred nodded. "Well, those guys were members of Antifa, and one of them had an outstanding warrant. After questioning him, he said they sold bomb-making materials to an older guy. We naturally assumed it was someone, say, in your father's age group." The chief was walking around the office as he spoke almost like he was giving a lecture. Fred looked up nodding, indicating he remembered. Harrison stopped and looked at Fred. "Ya know, back in the day, late sixties, there was an antiwar protester named Abby Hoffman. You ever hear of him?" Fred nodded his head. "Well, Abby Hoffman said, 'never thrust anyone over thirty'. To these twenty-year-old Antifa guys, anyone over thirty is old."

Fred spoke up, "Pat, where you going with this? Do I have to take a taxi to get to the end of your story?"

The Chief was a little irritated with Fred's comment. "Hang on Fred, I'm making a point here. Anyway, the person we should've been looking for was in their thirties, not an old guy. The FBI profile we got recently proves that out. The profile indicates a Caucasian, in their thirties or forties. Recently that same Antifa guy was picked up on another outstanding warrant. He said he had information about the recent bombings that might interest us. We made a plea deal with him. This guy said that he just sold bomb-making material."

Fred looked surprised. "You made a deal based on that sketchy bit of information? Sounds like you got took."

"Fred, he said it was the same guy he sold material to the last time." Fred hesitated; he was processing this new information. He threw the folder on the desk.

"OK. So do a composite sketch of that guy and pass it around to all your men."

Chief Harrison picked up the folder and looked at Fred.

"You didn't read through all the information."

"Hell, I didn't have to Pat. You have some information, and a potential facial recognition from this Antifa guy. You're on your way. You don't need me for this. I'm in no way involved."

The Chief looked at him, "Your brother's name is listed in the folder."

Fred stood up quickly, "Wait a minute, you trying to implicate my brother?"

Roy had been sitting quietly. He looked at Fred. "Fred, we worked together for a number of years. During that time, I got to know about your brother and basically your family. John was a hothead, you know that. He rattled a lot of management cages, made accusations, got the union members riled up. He was seen at one of the bomb sites. Didn't he say that 'whoever planted those bombs should receive a metal'? Ya, he's a person of interest."

Fred snapped at Roy, "Oh for Christ's sake, he was letting off steam. At the time he thought the post office was responsible for our brother Joey's death. You might've done the same thing." Hell, even I was a person of interest, because of John's union activities, and he was my brother."

The Chief stepped closer to him, and in a soft voice said, "Take is easy Fred, calm down."

"CALM DOWN? You're basically accusing John of setting off the bombs."

Again, in a soft tone voice Harrison said, "Fred, there is enough circumstantial evidence that I could bring John in for questioning, even get a warrant to impound his vehicle to test for bomb residue. But, we thought it might be easier if you could talk with John. Have him come in and talk with us. Then we can eliminate him as a person of interest. It would be better all around."

Fred stood up; he knew what the Chief said was true. It is what he would do if he were running this case.

"Ok, I'll talk to my brother and see if he'll come in. However, I want a lawyer or myself in there, just in case."

Roy spoke up, "Just in case of what?"

Fred looked over at him, "I don't know, just in case, that's all." He turned and left Harrison's office.

"What'd ya think Roy? You think Fred will get his brother to come in?" the Chief asked.

Roy gave a sigh, "Fred's a straight shooter, he'll do what's right. He's in an awkward situation, he has his brother listed as a person of interest in a bombing case. Besides, like Fred said, the information we have describes half the young men and pickup trucks in Minneapolis. And, he's right about the maintenance guy identifying someone he saw in the dark. We can just talk to John and eliminate him as a suspect."

Driving away from Chief Harrison's office, Fred was unnerved. This can't be happening. One member of his family was accused of a bombing, and now another is suspected of the same thing. Fred couldn't wrap his head around this. He just came out from California to visit his mother. Now he's being sucked into a bombing case. Surely, he thought, events are unfolding to an uncomfortable level. Now he's tasked with his brother's possible involvement in the bombings.

Fred went back to his hotel and called Allie. They agreed to meet at the Starbucks off Hennepin Avenue South. He wanted to vent and get her thoughts on the situation. Allie walked in and found Fred. He smiled as she approached.

"Hi Allie, thanks for coming on such short notice." She took the chair next to him and hung her purse over the backrest.

"No problem, I was just doing some cleaning, and I was glad to have a reason to stop." Fred had already bought her a coffee. She picked it up and took a sip.

"So, what's up? I didn't expect you to call so soon."

He had both hands around his coffee mug. "Ah, crap, things are getting complicated."

She looked puzzled. "Like how?" Her first impression was that Fred had second thoughts about their involvement. She was ready for anything.

Fred wanted to come clean with his situation. "I had a meeting this afternoon with Roy Downing, and Chief Harrison."

Allie's body language showed one of relief. "What about?" she said.

"Well, you probably heard about the most recent bombing." Allie nodded. "Roy called me early this morning; I mean at two-thirty!"

"Two-thirty?"

"Ya, anyway he asked me to come down to the Minneapolis post office." He went on to explain what took place, plus the meeting earlier this afternoon. He elaborated on what Roy and the Chief suspected, that the Chief showed him the folder on compiled bombing information. Fred summed it up by saying, he now had to talk his brother into meeting with the Chief. He looked at Allie.

"What do'ya think? Should I get involved or let the Chief and Roy handle things by themselves? Will I be doing the right thing by persuading John to meet with them?"

Allie shifted in her chair. "Well, it seems to me that you're already involved. If for no other reason, than by association. You're his brother, family, and you're familiar with the cases. Seems to me it might go easy for John if you were involved. He'd feel better knowing someone is in his corner."

Fred looked around the coffee shop, then back at her.

"I know, I know. It's just that I thought I had escaped all of this when I moved away. I was living my life, had no worries. Didn't ya ever just want to get away? Start somewhere new. Allie, you'd love California, good weather, a really nice place. You should try it."

She looked at him, "Maybe I will someday."

He shrugged his shoulders. "Hell, I just wanted to come out here, see my mother, give her my support, and help her get better. Now I'm confronted with all of this." He moved his hand in a sweeping motion through the air as if to indicate the recent events.

Allie reached over and put her hand on his arm. "Fred, you can't change the past, it happened. Now you must deal with things as they come. You haven't done anything wrong. Perhaps you should do what they ask and let things fall where they may. But you are involved. John is your brother, he's family and needs your support. Yet, I think you already knew this and just wanted to hear it out loud."

Fred looked at Allie, smiled and thought, this woman is very perceptive. He leaned back in his chair and patted her hand.

"You're right. I didn't cause these events, but I have to deal with them. All I can do is be there for my brother."

Allie sipped her coffee and smiled. They got up and walked outside Starbucks where he gave her a quick kiss, and they separated. As Fred drove away, he knew he had to find his brother.

CHAPTER 26

Fred woke up at 9 a.m. Tuesday morning. Lying in bed, he felt a bit groggy from last night. When he left Allie, he went back to the Hilton. He could feel the tension of the day working on his shoulders; they were tight. He went into the hotel bar, and had a few drinks, which didn't ease the stress, so he went up to his room. He had opened the mini bar and made a drink. Nothing seemed to be relieving the stress. This morning he wished he hadn't drank. He remembered something his father had said. The first thing alcohol affects is your judgment. His father was right. One or two drinks may lead you to think you can have another. In the end, it accomplishes nothing, except to give you a headache and a vague memory. He got up, showered, shaved, dressed, and headed to the Hilton restaurant for breakfast. With a good meal in his stomach and a few cups of coffee under his belt, he felt a bit refreshed. It was close to eleven when he left the restaurant. His thoughts went to where he'd find his brother. He called John, but it went to voice mail. Then he called his mother to ask if John had been there, his mother answered no. With no set plan, Fred decided to arbitrarily hit those places he thought John might be at. He drove over to the VFW with no luck. Mac the bartender said he hadn't seen John in days. Fred tried Murphy's Bar with the same results. It was noon, and Fred thought perhaps John was at school, but he didn't know his brother's schedule. With no other choice, he decided to just drive over to John's house and wait. As he pulled into John's driveway, he noticed the garage door was not all the way down. He got up and walked to the garage. There he saw the dark blue pickup parked inside. He turned and looked at the house. Fred went to the back door, it was locked. He knocked, no answer so he went around to the front. Again, he knocked, no answer. He peaked in the window and saw a foot hanging off the couch. He knocked louder this time, still no answer. Fred felt uneasy thinking something might be wrong with his brother. This time he banged on the door and shouted John's name. Fred finally heard movement inside. It seemed like a long time before the door opened.

"Weeell, looks whoss com'ta visit."

"John! What the hell's up with you?"

In a slurred voice John replied. "Meee? Nuthin'. What's zups with yous?" He smiled.

"Holy shit John, you're drunk." Fred made his way through the half-opened door.

His brother was hanging onto the door as a crutch. "Nopes, I were drunks but nows I'm soberin' ups." He kept smiling.

"John, what the hell, it's only noon and you're trashed. What's going on?"

John shut the door and leaned against it. "Nuthins' going on, I just having a few drinks, thads all folks." He waved his arm in a large circle to indicate goodbye.

"Jesus John, you can barely stand up."

"Maybes, but I am standing." He smiled, and held his arms up with his palms open, as if to make a point.

"Damn it, I'm gonna make you some coffee." Fred walked into the kitchen. "Where do you keep the coffee can?"

John pointed at the lower cabinet, his hand wavering in a slow circle. Fred opened the coffee can and measured out some for the pot.

"I don't believe you, it's only noon and you're drunk." He was both upset and surprised at his brother.

John took a deep breath, shrugged his shoulders, and smiled, "Well, a guy has to have a hobby."

"It's not funny, John. Why aren't you at school anyways?"

"I tooks da days off. Has to gives the brains cells some rest." He pointed to his tilted head, and winked one eye. "Yees sirs, the brains cells needs their rest." He walked over and flopped on the couch.

Fred walked into the living room. "How long have you been like this?" He looked around. "Look at this place, it's a mess."

With his eyes half closed John said, "Cuppa days I guess, and the maid hasn't been in yet." He smiled again.

Fred looked at his brother, "Smart ass, huh?"

John contoured his lips, "Yup", his lips made a popping sound.

Fred shook his head, "Ya know, sometimes you can be a dumb ass."

John looked up, "Mmmmm, you think smart ass and dumb ass are related? Maybe they're brothers, huh? I mean they have the same last name." He stared at Fred and smiled. Fred was frustrated, he came here to talk with his brother and found him drunk. How the hell was he going to pull this off. He turned and went to get the coffee. By the time John was on his second cup, Fred felt it wasn't helping a bit. All he had now was a wide awake drunk. He spoke to him.

"Look, John... John! Pay attention." He put his hand on his brother's shoulder. "You have to listen; there's a situation you need to address." John was looking down at his coffee cup. "John, you hear me?"

In an irritated voice he said, "Ya, ya, situation.... need ta 'dress it. Whatever that means."   "

John, the postal inspectors and the St. Paul Chief of Police want to talk with you."

John looked up with eyes half closed. "What the hell they want to talk with me about?"

Fred shifted in his chair. He didn't quite know how to approach this. "It's about the postal bombings." John sat up as if he was sober. "What about the bombings?"

"Well, they have a few questions to ask you. Your name was in a folder. It had information about the last bombing, Dad, and some Antifa guys. Stuff like that." Although he started to act alert, John was still drunk. He held his cup with both hands and slowly shook his head back and forth.

"Da bastards! They wants me too, huh? They killed Joey, then Dad, and now they wants me?" He stood up and threw his cup across the kitchen, it shattered against the sink. This sudden outburst caught Fred off guard. He wiped the coffee that had spilled out of the cup off his shirt.

John wobbled as he stood there. "That post office of yours, kills this family. Joey's gone, Dad's gone, hell even you're gone. It destroyed whats we had. Mom's alone, and I'm nowhere." He stumbled and braced himself against the cabinets. "Going to school trying to rebuild my life, the post office did all that shit, with Joey's death."

Fred looked at John like it was the first time. "Wait a minute John, you know it wasn't the post office's fault. That guy Sparks, who worked with Joey, he told you that."

"Ya, well maybe they pays him off, makes him a sweet deal, huh. Did'ja ever think of that, dumb ass brother?"

Fred couldn't help but to think that there was something wrong with his brother. John's thinking wasn't rational.

John staggered into the living room. He opened a drawer and took out a bottle and opened it. Fred came in after him. "C'mon John, that's the last thing you need."

With the same hand he held the bottle, John pointed at his brother. "Don't, don't!" John paused slightly, wavering an arm in the air. "Tells me what I needs." He took a swig of the bottle and wiped his mouth with a forearm. "I'm done with everything. I'm gonna make the post office pay, dems' bastards."

"John, c'mon, you don't mean that. This can all be cleared up. Just go talk to the inspectors and the Chief, you'll be done with them. In a few days, we can put this all behind us. We can put to rest what Dad did, and how they might've expected you to be connected. It'll all be done."

John started laughing. He staggered over to the couch and fell onto it. Taking a long slug from the bottle, he looked at Fred, then put the bottle in his lap. His shoulders went limp, his head was low. In a soft voice he said.

"Dad didn't do it."

Fred was standing near him. "What? What did you say?"

In the same soft voice John repeated. "Dad didn't do it."

Fred got closer. He was confused, he felt he wasn't hearing John right. "Dad didn't do what? The bombing? Are you saying Dad didn't do the bombings?" John didn't answer. Fred cuffed him on the shoulder with the back of his hand. "Hey, I'm talking to you. Did you say Dad didn't do the bombings?"

John looked up at his brother, licked his lips, and tried to take another drink from the bottle. Fred swatted it out of his hand, and it slid when it hit the ground.

"Answer me!"

"Ya. Dads didn't do the bombings." Fred sat on the coffee table in front of John. "How do you know this? Where did'ja get your information?" John was silent. Fred felt the tension building up inside him, "Answer me, damn it! How do you know Dad didn't do it?" John looked straight at Fred and paused trying to focus his eyes......
"cuz I did it."

The rage came out of Fred. He grabbed his brother by the lapels, lifted him up, and threw him across the room. John tumbled over an easy chair, landing by an old-style cast-iron radiator, banging his head. Fred went over, pulled him back up and threw him in the easy chair. "You bastard. Why, why? You told me it was Dad. That you and he had an argument about the stuff you found in his basement. The bomb making stuff, the bombing articles. All of it." Fred was hanging onto John's lapels.

John shook his head. "Nooooo, I said Dad and I argued 'bout thuh stuff found in da basement. Dad found stuff I hid there. That's what's we was arguin' about. He was yellin 'bout right 'n wrong. That I hadta turn myself in."

"So, that was what Dad meant when he said he could've stopped it? That he was trying to fix it?"

"Ya, ya, he has a suspicion that it was me, but he didn't have the heart ta turn his son in ta the 'thorities."

Fred spoke, "But what about the old articles about the Ann Harbor University SDS groups? The New York bombings?"

John tried to get up, but Fred held him down. "I heard Mom and Dad talking about it years ago. I just googled it. Never thought I should mention it, and forgot about the articles."

Fred shook him. "But why the bombings? Why'ja do it?"

John's eyes got a fire in them, he acted almost sober. "'Cause they killed Joey, they killed our kid brother!" John made another attempt to get up. If he hadn't been drinking, he could have done it. Even though Fred was a bit taller, John was the strongest. But, being drunk, John didn't have a chance. Fred shook John again, yelling at him. "YOU LET DAD TAKE THE BLAME FOR WHAT YOU DID! And what about Mom? She has to live alone, with the shame, because of this."

John was still intoxicated and even with the conflict he wasn't thinking right. "Dad was an old man; his heart gave out. It could've happened any day."

Fred shook him again. John grabbed Fred's arms.

"Will ya stops 'zat?"

Fred looked down at John. "Ya, Dad had a heart attack at the damn post office. What was he doing there?" John resigned to the fact that he wasn't going anywhere and slumped in the easy chair.

"What was Dad doing at the post office that night?" John didn't answer, so Fred shook him.

John said, "For Christ' Sake quit doin' that."

"I'll shake the teeth out of your head if you don't answer me."

John looked at him. "Dad knew I planted a bomb, and he went ta get it. He grabbed that old bag he used to carry fireplace wood in. He said he was gonna go get the bomb. I have to admit, he was one feisty som'bitch."

Fred held up a fist over John, "I swear to God, one more comment like that, and I'll beat the hell out of ya. Now why didn't ya stop him?"

"I tried. I told him I'd go get the bomb. He settled down and that was that."

Fred stood up after letting go of John. "But you had no intention of retrieving the bomb, did ya?"

The fire came back into John's eyes, "No, no I wasn't, they were gonna pay for what they did to Joey, and what they did to this family. I wanted the post office to pay just like this family paid. I'd do it again and again." Dad probably knew that and went to get it himself."
In a calmer voice Fred said, "So even when you sat in my car that night, you didn't care that Dad was in danger?"
"Noooo, that's not it." John started to sob. "After you got out of the car, I went to get Dad. I knew where he might be. I was going to get him, the bomb, and get us out of there. Then he goes and has a heart attack. I never saw that coming, never thought it would happen." John gently sobbed. "Ya gotta believe me on that, Fred. I loved Dad and would not've wanted anything to harm him." Then the fire came back to John's eyes. "But the post office had to pay and that's why I started doin' it again." Just as quick as it came, the fire was gone.
Fred looked down at his brother. "You're a sick man John, you don't see what you've done, and you're blaming others. You need help."
John stood up wobbling, "Sick man my ass. You're the sick one, letting them do our family like that." He stumbled and fell back into a chair. He banged his fist against the easy chair cushion and sobbed.
Fred shook his head, pulled out his cell phone and called the Chief.

CHAPTER 27

The clinking of the ice in his drink was familiar. The Jameson was tasting good, and he was enjoying the warmth of the sun on his face. The Bamber Breeze rocked gently, almost lulling him to sleep. Even the squawking of the seagulls was comforting. All of this was disrupted by something suddenly blocking the sun. It cast a shadow over him. He put a hand to his eyes to block the glare and looked up. There was a figure standing near the boat.

"Buy me a drink sailor?" It was a familiar voice that brought an immediate smile to his face.

"Allie?" Fred moved to get a better look. She was smiling, "What the hell! What are you doing out here?"

"Well, you once said I'd love California. So, I thought I'd see what it's all about, and here I am."

He got up and went to the side of the boat. "Ya, but I never really thought you'd do it."

She challenged him, "Hey, look it, I can turn around."

Fred stammered, "No, no, what I meant was…. ahhh, I mean I didn't think you would …ahh, hell I don't know what I meant. I guess I didn't think you were listening to me, after all I was kinda rambling on that night." Smiling, he reached out his hand to her, "Well, hey, c'mon aboard, and try out your sea legs." With his hand for support, she climbed over the boat railing into the Bamber Breeze.

"Damn, you look great Allie," He stood there smiling, his hands on his hips, his stance had his legs apart, like a pirate. "It's great to see ya."

"Well, you don't act like it."

Fred's face went deadpan, his smile disappeared, and he looked quizzical. "Whaat? Why'd ya say that?"

Now she had a slight smile, "Well you could give me a hug, ya big jerk." His face lit up with a smile. He reached over, picked her up, and gave her a big bear hug.

"Ok, ok," she protested, as she tried to catch her breath, "That's a bit too much."

He put her down and stood there with a childish smile on his face as if he'd just accomplished something. He was happy.

"Seriously Allie, it's great to see you."

She made the motions of straightening out any wrinkles caused by the hug. She then put her hand on his chest, "It's good to see you too, Fred." She walked over and sat down in one of the two deck chairs. "So, what does a girl have to do to get a drink on this boat?"

Fred acted startled, like he just remembered he had something to do. "Oh, ya, ya let me fix you a drink. Vodka tonic, ok?" He started to make his way to the cabin as she answered.

"Vodka tonic will be fine."

Fred made the drink, came back out and handed it to Allie. "Here'ya go." He sat down in the other chair and took a sip of his Jameson. "So, tell me all about how you just decided to come out here." He leaned back in his chair and placed one foot on the boat railing.

She looked at him. "Well, don't you remember? You gave me a sort of invite. After things settled down in Minneapolis.... say wait a minute, I have a bone to pick with you." Allie leaned forward, "What the hell do you mean just taking off like that? No goodbye, no 'hey Allie I'm heading back to California'. I have no idea what took place after I saw you that last time. You could've had the decency to see me before you left, you owed me that much. And what the hell happened? Roy wouldn't talk much about it. He just said they put your brother away and you took off." Her voice was tense, she stood up, and she was angry now. "I thought you at least cared something about me, but.......nooooo. You just took off like a thief in the night. I don't even know why the hell I came out here." She headed to the side of the boat to get off.

He got up and blocked her path. "Allie, wait, wait. You're right, I handled this all badly. Allie, please, sit down, I'll tell you everything. Please?"

She hesitated, still upset, she was a bit unsure of her feelings. Yet, she wanted to know what made him abruptly leave Minneapolis. She turned and walked back to her chair and sat down. She looked at him. "This better be goddamn good, Fred!" Allie stared at him.

Fred sat down next to her. He was taking the time to process all his information, to explain it the best he could. He saw that Allie was angry with him, but more important to him was her emotional demeanor. This was more than just taking off. She had let herself get personally involved with him. He realized he owed her an explanation, and yes, he better make it good. He was slowly rubbing his palms together in a circular motion. He was looking down at them, then looked up, and looked into her eyes.

"Allie, there's no amount of words that can explain how sorry I am for the way I left. And yes, it bothered me. This month has not been easy. I've thought about you a lot. I'd be sitting here wishing you were with me." Allie leaned back in her chair. She was trying to figure out where this was going.

Fred spoke, "I guess the best way is to go back to the last night I was with John." Fred described how he found John drunk. That, John, eventually confessed that it was him who set the bombs off. How he allowed their father to take the blame, and it ate away at him. It gnawed at his insides. For some reason, John kept going back to blaming the post office for the deaths of Joey and our father. He became obsessed with it. I have to admit Allie, I came close to beating the hell out of my brother." Fred continued, "After I called the Chief, they came and took him away. I was dumbfounded. I sat on John's couch and didn't know what to do. I thought, how can this be happening to my family? A solid middle-class family, never any problems, a good Midwestern family. I eventually had to tell my mother. The strange thing was, that, she was that other woman again. Not Mom, not the mother I knew growing up, but that solid, in control woman who appeared the night my father died. Well, anyways, John was interrogated, but Chief Harrison saw something. He called in a psychiatrist. The doctor described John as suffering from PTSD. He said John was acting out latent emotions because of Joey's death. That John was not looney, that for him, the line between right and wrong was blurred."

Allie spoke up, "But why did the Chief decide to call in a psychiatrist?"

"Well, remember when I said that the Chief was 'old school'?"

"Ya but..."

Fred talked over her, "He said he'd seen this on more than one case back in New York. That there was something he remembered that triggered a request for a psychiatric evaluation. All I can say is thank God for old school thinking. Anyways, John was committed to a psychiatric hospital for treatment."

Allie leaned forward, "Wow, seems like the Chief was looking out for your family."

Fred looked at her, "No, I just think he's just a great cop."

"But Fred, what about your mother? Surely she was devastated by all of this."

"Not really Allie. Let me tell you, I'll never underestimate that woman ever! She showed me more grit, more moxie than any person I ever met. I mean, there she is, her family dissolving before her, and she was spot on with her response, clear, concise, practical."

"Hold on, Fred." Allie said. "She may have held her chin high when things were falling around her, but as a mother, as a woman, at night she cried. The momma bear in her came out, she protected her family in the best way she could, but at night she suffered."

Fred knew he was out of his element. He had no idea about woman's psyche, so he let it pass.

"So, Fred what did your mother do?"

"Well, after John's sentence to treatment, I tried to talk my mother into moving out to California so I could assist her. Be with her in a warm climate."

Allie laughed, "I'm sorry Fred, but from the way you described your mother, that must have gone over like a lead balloon."

Fred looked down a bit and smiled, "Ya, well you got me there. In not so many words, she told me, 'Why should I leave Minnesota'? She grew up there, and knew lot'sa people? No! She was tired of the house and yard work, but she was not giving up. She decided to move to an assisted living facility, where she had friends. There was Sven and his wife, Jack and his wife plus a number of others. No thank you, she said, I got this covered. That's what she said, I've got this covered. Go beat that."

Allie looked at him.

"All this doesn't explain why you left without so much as a phone call." Fred was on the spot, he knew it, and knew that his explanation was not going to be good enough. He took both of her hands in his, looked at her and spoke.

"Allie. I believe my reason will not satisfy you, but its real. I was embarrassed, it's as simple as that. No, it was more than that, I was ashamed. I had a brother killed in an industrial accident, a father died on a post office dock, a brother convicted of bombing the post office. I guess I felt that it was a bit too much for anybody to accept. My family would forever be associated with the postal bombings. So, I thought I'd just cut ties, be done with it. Yet even now, they sound like stupid reasons to me."

She looked at him, "And you never considered giving me the opportunity to choose?"

"Ahhhh no. C'mon Allie, guys are not good at that."

She hit back fast, "Well maybe you should be! Maybe you should get over your macho bull and consider others."

"Look Allie, I know you're angry, and you have a right to be angry."

She cut him off, "You're damn right I'm angry!" Then Allie paused, and in a calmer, softer voice she said, "No Fred, I'm beyond angry. I'm disappointed in you. I felt we had started something we both wanted, but now I think perhaps it was just a stopover for you. I thought you were better than that." She turned and looked out at the ocean.

Fred sat there. He wasn't sure how to respond. He looked at her and he felt despondent. "You're right, Allie. Everything you've said is right. In a way, I'm disappointed in myself at how I handled things. I just wanted an easy path to get away from all that conflict in Minneapolis." She turned back around and looked at him. "You know Fred, sometimes the easiest path can be the most torturous." She looked out over the marina. "Maybe it was a mistake coming out here. I just wanted an answer as to why you left without at least saying goodbye. I got an answer, not the best, but at least I know. There's nothing more for me than to go back." She moved to get off the Bamber Breeze.

Fred stood up quickly. He put his hands on each of her arms, "Allie, wait, please don't go. Look, I can't undo what's done. I've handled things badly, acted irrational, I'm aware of this. But I don't want us to end. For the past month I thought of you a lot. I missed your company," I.... missed being with you, I missed everything about you. Don't go. You're here, let me show you that I am that 'better man' you thought I was. I don't want you to go. I don't want to sit here wishing I had tried to stop you from leaving. Allie, I want to be with you. I want us to be together."

Allie looked up at him, her eyes started to tear, and she began to smile. "Ya big jerk. Why couldn't have said that in the beginning? I don't want us to end either. But I just need to know that you'll at least invest yourself emotionally to make this work. I need that, Fred."

He looked at her and said, "I 'll do whatever it takes, I want us to be together."

The boat rocked gently as they stood on the Bamber Breeze holding each other.

Fate had finally made things right.

THE END